LOVE, Mercy

CODE OF HONOR SERIES
BROOKE MAY

Love, Mercy
Copyright © 2019, Brooke May

Printed in The United States of America.
ISBN 9781698813301
First Edition

Edited by Editing4Indies
Cover Art by Dark Water Covers

This book is a work of fiction. Names, characters, places, and incidents are the product of the author's imagination or are used fictitiously. Any resemblance to actual events, locales, or persons, living or dead, is coincidental.

All Right Reserved. No part of this publication may be reproduced, distributed, or transmitted in any form of by any means, including photocopying, recording, or other electronic or mechanical methods, without the prior written permission of the author, except in case of brief quotations embodied in critical reviews and certain other noncommercial uses permitted by copyright law. For permission requests, write the author.

In accordance with the U.S. Copyright Act of 1979, the scanning, and electronic sharing of any part of this book without the permission of the publisher or author constitute piracy and theft of the author's intellectual property. If you would like to use material from this book (other than for review purpose), prior written permission must be obtained by contacting the publisher at bmay3129@gmail.com. Thank you for your support of the author's rights.

FBI Anti-Piracy Warning: The unauthorized reproduction of distribution of a copyrighted work is illegal. Criminal copyright infringement, including infringement with monetary gain, in investigated by the FBI and is punishable by up to five years in federal prison and a fine of $250,000.

To the Men and Women of our Armed Forces; past, present, and future.

Prologue

IT WASN'T INSTANTANEOUS.

It wasn't a moment that had my heart stopping, my breath freezing in my lungs, my soul searing to his when our gazes locked, and it most certainly wasn't love at first sight.

The day I met Daxon Logan, I was about to knock a fifth grader out for picking on me and my friend, Angelica. My fist almost went into his cute face instead, but he was bigger and was able to stop me from even fully extending my arm toward the older boy.

I was a fourth grader, a year younger and far smaller than either of them. It didn't stop me from putting Daxon in his place, though. I laid into him, telling him I was perfectly capable of handling my own battles and that I didn't need a boy to step in.

Little did my younger self know, the boy before me would play a larger part in my life.

Brooke May

Our friendship wasn't something instant or constant after that point. Daxon had his own friends and life to lead while the same could be said for me. Our parents had become friends. Our fathers served in Vietnam together and were reunited after Daxon's family moved to Centennial. Their friendship grew strong, and our mothers became close. That meant Daxon was around a lot after our initial meeting.

Our friendship was finite. We remained strictly friends until everything began to change for me during the summer after my sophomore year of high school. I no longer saw Daxon as a boy with a hero complex who always wanted to step in and rescue someone—mainly me. He was no longer the boy who was the only one willing to take me serious on the playground when I wanted to play soldiers rather than hang out on the monkey bars and pretend I was a gymnast. He was the only boy who thought my dream of becoming a soldier like my dad was great.

I had spent the entire summer watching him through the dark lenses of my shades. I grew tongue-tied and sweaty, and my pulse was irate whenever he was close to me. I learned my body's reaction to him was something deeper than I could truly understand, and I didn't particularly care for it at first. I was the

Love, Mercy

tough girl, the one who never shied away from conflict and who was more comfortable being around boys.

My observations lasted only for those three months before I had finally mustered up enough of my ever-present courage to ask him out at the beginning of my junior year.

He was starting his senior year, and he said yes.

We went through thick and thin that year. Girls trying to steal him was our main issue. I was always seen as the little sister type or one of the guys, so there was never a worry about a guy hitting on me. At least in my mind. It also helped that most guys were terrified of me, but Daxon was still very diligent about who was around me.

When he told me he was going to join the Army and follow in our fathers' footsteps I was thrilled for him. It was a dream that both of us shared, and I planned on joining him a year later.

I couldn't wait for the opportunity to serve my country alongside the man I loved.

We were kids filled with dreams, and sometimes, those dreams just don't come true.

Daxon was there the day I went to the recruiter. To say excitement pulsated around us was an understatement. We talked about the world that would be opened up to us as we drove there. He held my hand as we walked into the building and cradled me to his gradually growing chest as we left. He soaked up my tears after I was told the twist in my spine would never allow me to join any branch of the military. Even if I were to have surgery to correct it, the possibility of joining was still slim.

And like the few other times, I was left in tears—which was rare—Daxon did what he always did best and replaced my sorrow with joy. He took me on a hike, and even with the brisk air beating around us, I didn't feel the cold. I was led to an overlook we had run to whenever we had the opportunity to get to in the mountains over our home. The wind was strong, the scent of fall filled our lungs, and the view was spectacular as he sank to one knee and asked me to be his forever.

I have never regretted saying yes.

I didn't envy Daxon for living his dream while I was left behind. Instead, I focused on being the best supportive wife I could be to him. With each tour that took him away, I knew we were okay. I was left to plan our wedding for the following year while he

Love, Mercy

was in Iraq for the first time. Care packages were sent as often as I could put them together for him and I was the first person to greet him, when he stepped off the plane.

We wrote our own vows. Mine were written on a tear-spotted paper while his were on a worn sheet he kept close to him throughout his tour.

I loved the man I married, and I love his duty to his country. I was honored to call him my husband as well as my hero and learned to admire his hero complex that he never quite got rid of. I knew that no matter where he was in the world or what he was doing, I was always one of the first thoughts he had when he woke up and the last when he was able to get a decent night's sleep.

This isn't your typical romance story.

Chapter One

LIGHT PRESSURE GLIDES AGAINST my legs and then vanishes, only to appear a little higher up on my thigh.

"Mmm, that feels so good." My body wants to stretch, but I won't. Not with the delectable weight of my husband on top of me and his heat warming my uncovered body.

"Not as nice as you feel." His lips dance across my naked flesh as puffs of air send sensations throughout my body. "Good morning, babe."

"Good morning." My eyes flutter open; the benefit of my lack of make up the day before makes the move easier than if I had yesterday's mascara crusting around my lids. Instead of reaching above my head to pop my arched back, my fingers find their way into the short hair on the top of Daxon's head. He hasn't had anything longer than the required military cut since high school. I love it this way. It means I get to see more of his face and handsome build as I look down at his massive body.

Love, Mercy

Tightly packed muscles from rigorous workouts and skin pulled taut over those fierce cuts cage my legs under him as he slowly creeps his naked perfection up my lounging body.

"You. Are. So. Beautiful. Mercy." He speaks between kisses, and my stomach tightens as it comes to life with flutters. No matter how many times I'm close to this soldier and hear the words in his deep timbre, I feel like the giddy schoolgirl I was when I first asked him out.

"I love how you wake me up." We don't have to have sex to be intimate. It's like breathing between him and me; an ease for us to have this deep and satisfying connection. Not that the sex isn't mind-blowing each time, but I love just being near him.

"And I love how responsive you are to me." Finally, his strong jaw is level with my rounder one. Leaning forward, he envelops mt naked body with his warmth as his lips press against mine. Tender and nearly to the point of tears, he kisses me. It shows how much love he has for me.

I know he dotes on me as much as possible because our little bubble is about to burst. Our time is drawing to an end … for now. Duty is calling him away once more, and I long to keep the clock hands from moving even half of a second just so I can hold onto this time with him a little while longer.

All too soon, our kiss is broken, but he pauses before he moves away. I know he senses what I have passed from my lips to his. The darkness in his already dark gray eyes reflects the sadness slowly consuming me.

"I don't want you to go." I feel so selfish stating this. I know better than anyone what his career entails.

He gets off the bed, and my gaze fixates on the firm globes of his toned ass.

Yes, perfection.

And he's all mine. Every time I see him, clothed or naked, I feel the need to pinch myself to make sure this isn't just a teenage dream. And thankfully, it isn't. Daxon Ray Logan is all mine.

"Mercy, you know I can't back out." There is no note of irritation in his voice.

"I know." Rolling onto my stomach, I don't bother to cover my nudity. We are in the privacy of our little home I had to find by myself and then email to him to make sure it was what we both wanted. His duty will always take him away until he is ready to retire and step away from all of it. We are still in our twenties, so he is far from retiring from what he loves doing. And I understand that the Army will always be a mistress in our relationship.

But I adore his honor.

At the threshold of the en suite bathroom, Daxon turns to me. Every solid muscle in his tall body is on display as he braces himself against the doorframe. His arms cross, and my eyes lock onto the strong yet delicate tattoo of my name on his forearm and the Army symbol on the other.

"Our country needs me, babe."

"I understand." My shoulders fall. I am a strong woman, but sometimes it is a little too much to be strong when the one person I love more than my own life isn't by my side every night.

For his build, he is incredibly quiet as he quickly closes the distance between us. I'm lifted with ease off the bed and cradled into his arms. His nose pressed against mine. I don't mind the morning breath as he speaks. The heat of his wide eyes fills me with honesty as his grip around me reinforces the strength of his words.

"I promise you, Mercy Jessica Logan, that no matter what situation I find myself in, I will *always* find my way back to you. I love you so much."

"And I love you."

Daxon,

I hope this email finds you safely. I wasn't sure what way to write to you. Normally, emails have worked just fine for us, but seeing as everything has changed, I decided to give this a try before resorting to putting you through the torture of attempting to read my handwriting.

I miss you. As if you didn't already know that, but it's as true as the first time I ever said it. I'm doing okay. Work is slowly picking up. We aren't in a popular energy area in the state, as you know, but I have enough to keep me busy.

I went to our spot last week to celebrate our anniversary early. It wasn't the same without you by my side but I knew that wherever you were, you were thinking of me at the same time as I was looking up at the blue sky and seeing your handsome face.

Our dads have decided to take up black powder shooting. They were watching something the other day and decided they needed it as a hobby. Our mothers are *thrilled*. Can you sense my sarcasm? I know you can. You know me too well. Anyway, they are working on building their own guns and then are going to attempt to put a club together. This should be interesting.

Brooke May

I guess that's all I have for now. I hope you are safe and that this reaches you soon. I can't wait to hear from you.

Love,

Mercy

Mercy,

As much as I would love to see your fabulous handwriting, see I can do sarcasm too, emails are the best bet to reach me for the time being. Everything is going as well as can be expected and that's all I am at liberty to say, even to you. For that, I'm sorry.

I miss you, too. I have this picture of you in my mind I wish I had a hard copy of. But then again, it's a full-frontal nude, and I don't really want the guys to see you in a state only allowed for my eyes. Maybe if I can get you an address for a care package, you can send me a picture of you in something sexy like one of my shirts or something?

I'm glad work is keeping you busy and I'm sorry I couldn't be there for our anniversary, but as you said, I was thinking of you. The sand has nothing on the mountains, but my imagination works well enough to fill in that void.

As for our dads, good for them! Those two need something to do on the weekends. Keep me posted on the progress they make with their guns. I hope they don't mess up and end up blowing themselves up like they almost did with their homemade cannon.

Brooke May

I don't have much more time on the computer. I can't wait to hear more from you, babe.

I love you,

Daxon

Chapter Two

BEING A MILITARY WIFE isn't something to take lightly.

The hours, days, and months of loneliness can be debilitating at times. Being unsure of your future with your husband can leave you feeling on edge and lead to anxiety issues every time you turn on the news and see something has happened where your man is supposed to be. It's even worse when you don't know where he is because he isn't allowed to share that information with you.

But each time he walks through those doors or steps off a plane, you cherish and embrace the rare moments he is on loan to you from the government. You fill those times with as much love and great memories as you can before you lose him again, and you're okay with that. Yet you kid yourself that he is completely yours until he is gone once more.

I've been through this process three times after we got married.

I have had plenty of me time to complete my degree in environmental biology and get a great job at an energy consulting firm for this part of Montana. To fill the giant Daxon-sized void in my life, volunteered at the VFW. I spent time there after working all day, I didn't feel *as* lonely by the time I got home.

I did end up welcoming another male into our home to keep me company when I hit an all-time low during Daxon's second tour. It was longer, and I felt isolated.

No, I'm not one of those women who run around on her man when he is away fighting for our country. I'm talking about a little guy who has a permanent black eye and is mostly white with tan and black spots on his back and legs.

Trigger was a gift to myself when the loneliness became too much. I had gone from a constant of Daxon in my life to barely speaking to him. Sure, I had our family but they couldn't be with me all the time at home. Trigger is an adorable Australian sheep dog I found at the local shelter after I started volunteering there on the weekends.

He's been my constant, and Daxon absolutely loves him.

Love, Mercy

Yet sometimes even his companionship isn't enough to fight off the loneliness, which leads me to where I am tonight.

After work, I was on my way home when my friend Angie called me and suggested we head to the bar for a couple of drinks. It had been a while since I've been out, so I agreed to come out for a drink and something to eat. It beat the alternative of going home to make a meal for one and then watch mindless episodes of a random show until it was time for bed.

I thought it would be fun to catch up with her and her friend Patience, who is slowly becoming one of mine and it was until Angie's single status won out over our friendship and Patience's rounded belly caused her to call it an early night. And now I'm left to deal with the pain in the ass currently sitting next to me.

My wedding ring, though simple, has always been on full display since the moment Daxon slipped it onto my finger. The symbol of our love is something I can't live without when he isn't with me. Yet men still think they are welcome to hit on me.

No matter how many times I tell them off and then get mean about how they have absolutely nothing enticing for me, they don't get it.

"Come on, love, just one dance." His words are close to being slurred.

My nose wrinkles up as I look out at the bar behind us. The dance floor is mostly empty on this weeknight. Instead, sports are playing on the TVs that the owner is slowly installing around the building. I'm not in the mood for dancing. Not that I ever am. I'm not the dancing type.

And besides, if I were forced to dance, there is only one man aside from my dad who I would be willing to shuffle around with.

"Please, go away." If he notices the bite to my words, he doesn't let on. *Didn't his parents ever teach him that no means no?*

"Come on." If this is the only line he has, he is wearing it out far too quickly. I'm so over dealing with this man.

"No," I growl. Turning away from him, I take in the game playing on the TV over the bar. I don't care that it's golf because I just want this man to go away.

"You can't possibly know what you are talkin' about." A hand wraps around my wrist. My fists instantly clench as I ready to

Love, Mercy

lay this man out. I know the owner, and I know well enough that he would never throw me out if I get into a fight with this guy.

"Go. Away." Since he's clasped my left hand, I'm going to have to hit him with my right, which works for me since it's my stronger arm. But just as I'm about to swing, a large wall is put up between the offending idiot and me. I'm pissed at the intrusion, but at least I'm free.

And now I have to deal with yet another man, but one who thinks he needs to rescue me.

Pulling in a lung full of air, I'm ready to berate the man when a familiar scent slams into me. My legs turn to jelly, my heart races, pulse quickens, and a thrill shoots through every nerve in my body.

Chapter Three

I'M SLOW ON THE UPTAKE.

Seconds tick by slowly as realization starts to settle into my mind. I know it isn't the amount of alcohol I've consumed tonight. I've only had a single beer, and I nursed it while I ate my hamburger and fries at dinner.

The smell wafting off the man who is giving me his back debilitates me in the most wonderful of ways, and I have missed that.

I know this massive back better than I know my own body. I know the American flag tattoo that spans from one shoulder to the other and what it feels like under my fingertips as I hold him tightly.

"D-Daxon?"

His name stumbles out of my mouth as if I'm the drunk in this scenario. Tears begin to pool in my eyes. They burn and well up to the point that I need to blink, but I don't want to. I'm afraid if I do, I may lose him. He may be a figment of my imagination.

Love, Mercy

Something I have conjured up to help me rid myself of this annoying man who doesn't understand being turned down.

Before I can think better of it, including the possibility of launching myself at the man I was just trying to get rid of, I hurl myself into the strong back. There is no doubt that the scent is that of *my* man.

"Oh, Daxon." I sob, filled with so much happiness that he is here. I nuzzle my way closer to him, taking in the ever-present heat that he always radiates. I wasn't sure when he would be able to come home again.

After his first tour, he was moved to special ops and gets pulled away more often than his first position ever did. It takes him away from him in infrequent intervals, and I always worry about him a little more because he can't tell me anything other than he is okay.

"You're here," I murmur as I'm forced to release him and step back so he can turn to face me. The stoic expression isn't one I was expecting to see. Normally, he is full of smiles and has no qualms about the fact he is happy to see me.

"You weren't home." His deep voice to anyone else would imply that he is disappointed, but I know him better than he knows himself. He is just making an observation, but he is still thrilled to have me within reaching distance again.

My shoulder hikes up because I have nothing to apologize for. "The girls wanted to meet up."

"I can see that." A solid finger tucks under my chin, lifting my gaze to his. I have no issue staying fixated on his massive chest, but taking in his handsome, strong-jawed face is something I fawn over. "Hi, babe."

"Hi, handsome." I don't bite back my smile. I'm overjoyed at seeing my husband. But I can't forget about the man I was just dealing with. "You didn't need to help me. I was handling him."

"Yeah." He doesn't believe me. Or he does but doesn't want to bother even thinking about the other man. "I didn't feel that it would be much fun to collect you from the sheriff's office."

"Duke would have let me off on a warning if Holt's old man even called them."

"Duke is only a deputy, and Holt's dad would have started placing bets on how long it would take you to make the man cry." When he pulls me to him, all other conversation fades away when his lips capture mine. I don't care that we are in public. My arms wrap around his corded neck, dragging him down closer to me. His massive hands my hips, anchoring our bodies together as I give him just as much as he returns.

He tastes so good. Like crisp spring water after a long, hot hike. God, I've missed this man.

"I wanted to surprise you." He pulls away, but only a breath is between us. "But that didn't pan out, and I had to go search for you."

"I'm unpredictable. You know this well." I'm breathy; I want more of him. I want his lips to return to mine.

"Yeah, it makes it a massive pain in the ass to surprise you like you wish I would do after you watch all those YouTube videos."

"Well, how about we go back to my place, and you can show me how much you've missed me?"

"Your husband isn't home?"

"Not at the moment, but I'm more than willing to rectify that." Pulling a twenty out of my purse, I slide it across the bar to one of the bartenders and then grab Daxon as I lead him out of the bar.

Chapter Four

IT HAS NEVER BEEN this difficult before to unlock the front door.

Daxon's lips are on my neck. My hands tremble as I attempt once more to slide the key into the lock. I have to grab the doorknob with my other hand in a failing effort to stabilize myself to unlock it.

I'm overzealous for this moment.

My car was left behind at the Grizzly. Daxon didn't give me a choice. He scooped me up in his big strong arms and ate up the pavement to his truck in long strides. My hands were all over him on the drive back to our little home. And now was his turn to reciprocate.

Just as his large hands wrap around my waist and his fingers begin to brush against the smallest hint of my exposed flesh as he tries to dive into the front of my slacks, I get the door open.

Turning around, wrap my arms around his neck once more, and my lips seal over his as I drag him into the darkened depths of our home. I want to crawl up this man like no other.

Love, Mercy

Once past the threshold, Daxon kicks the door shut. One hand abandons my waist so he can reach behind him and lock it. We may not live in a big city, but there are still occasional break-ins.

My purse tumbles to the floor, and I kick off my heels with reckless abandon while I work his shirt free from his jeans. I'm so consumed by him that I back us right into the couch.

And then a thought hits me. It takes everything in me to free my lips from Daxon's.

"Wait, Trigger."

"He's in the laundry room." He leans into me, causing my back to dig into the back of the couch. "I put him in there when I came here first to surprise you." His kisses are hungry against my neck. I'm lifted onto the couch, my legs spreading with ease to accommodate his larger frame.

"Good thinking."

I pant, my head falling back to grant him access to my neck and my back arches as the buttons of my shirt are gently released, exposing my black lace bra.

"I didn't want him to eat the flowers I brought you," he mumbles. Those glorious lips of his skim across the swell of my breasts with each word.

"Oh." I moan. He doesn't have enough hair for me to grab so my fingers dig into the fabric of his tight shirt instead.

The cool air of the room doesn't have a chance to even touch me because his warmth is instantly there. His hard, taut body fits perfectly against mine as he kisses me on the lips once more. Our tongues duel with one another. My shirt is removed. My bra doesn't last much longer after that. His heated hand splays out across my back, supporting me as I lean back.

"I've missed you so fucking much, Mercy." He growls into my mouth before he is gone.

Watching under hooded eyes as this powerful man sinks to a crouch between my legs is thrilling. My heart rate doubles, my breathing hitches, my nipples pebble, and my lower muscles clench at the knowledge of what is to come.

"I've missed you, too," I whisper as I lift my butt enough to allow him to free me from my slacks and matching black lace thong.

Love, Mercy

"Fuck, Mercy." He growls. "Knowing you wear this when you don't know I'm going to be home is going to make it difficult *not* to get hard when I leave again."

Ice shoots into my chest with the thought his words provoke. I don't want to think about him leaving again. Not here, not now.

"I like the thought of you thinking about me."

"I know you do, babe." I'm completely bare; he's still clothed, but that line of thought goes out the goddamn window as his hands spread me wider, and he skims his way up my inner thigh until he reaches my apex. "So fucking much."

I feel his lopsided grin against my flesh before he places a kiss on my glistening pussy. I'm gone at the simple touch.

"Oh, Daxon."

He says no more. His talented mouth does enough of that as he first nibbles on my throbbing clit. My pussy is clenching and growing needier. I'm overwhelmed with sensations that I haven't felt since the last time he was home.

Giving myself pleasure will never amount to what this man can do to me.

I brace myself on the couch, doing my best not to fall backward onto the cushions below. My fingers dig into the fabric of his shirt while I imagine it is his strong shoulders instead. I want to mark him before he leaves me again. I nearly jump off the couch and onto his face when his tongue spears into my core. His growls vibrate through my body, bringing me that much closer to my release.

I love how he tends to me first, and since it has been a while, it doesn't take me long before stars begin shooting in my gaze, and I scream out his name. And then I am falling. My back lands on the cushions, my legs are up in the air, and I have no time to process what is happening because seconds after I open my eyes, I'm gifted with a rushed but enchanting strip show.

Quickly, I right myself, my body falling into the plush cushions once more and deeper into the couch he can't stand, I watch as my present unwraps itself. His muscles ripple and move as he pulls his shirt over his head, and then they bunch while he works the buckle, button, and zipper of his jeans. He is bare underneath. No underwear means he can come back to me sooner.

Love, Mercy

I may not understand why he doesn't like to wear any underwear, but I'm not going to question him now.

My post-orgasmic bliss leads straight back to thrill as he stalks over to me.

"You are perfection, Mercy." His deep timbre has me squirming.

"You aren't bad yourself." My head tilts back to keep my gaze with him as he leans forward and I am once more in his arms. My legs wrap around his waist, and we turn so I am on top of him. His steely length nestles between my folds, but that *isn't* where I want him.

We haven't used a condom since before we were married. And I'm not on any form of birth control either. If a pregnancy happens, it happens, and we will embrace and love that child like no other. Once he is seated, I lift my body and help guide him into my body.

Slowly, I sink, filling every inch of my pussy with him. There is nothing more perfect than to have us joined like this.

Daxon's head falls back as a groan erupts from him. I wait a moment, soaking it up before I begin to move. As I gyrate over him, using the strength in my legs to rock my body, Daxon's hands roam my body. He cups my breasts, kissing them, licking and sucking each in turn before he reaches down to cup my ass.

My thrusts are slow and steady and then quick and reckless as I get closer to my next release. Daxon isn't too far off either. My body falls apart over him, my inner muscles clenching him to the point that even the rest of my body can't move.

Yearning for his release now, Daxon is off the couch and flips me onto it before he begins to thrust into my body wildly. My legs loosen and are lifted over his strong shoulders as he drives into me at a relentless pace.

My body is jostled and brought back up to another high. I fall apart, my body going lax at the same time that he roars.

Silence follows; my breathing is shallow and barely audible. My eyes droop until they close. They don't open when he bends down and picks me up. My arms are noodles as I drape them over his shoulders on our way to our room.

Chapter Five

CCALLING INTO WORK ISN'T something I do all too often. Even when I don't feel well, I drag myself into the office because it beats sitting around my house with a dog who tries to eat my used tissues.

Today is an exception.

Today, I'm spending the day with my husband so I can have a three-day weekend with him. Neither one of us knows how long he will be home, so I plan on using all the time I can. If I hadn't already put in for my vacation days this year, I would have taken them this week to be near him.

I don't want to leave him for any period of time. That includes going to work for a few hours during the weekdays. As much as it saddens me, I can't press pause on my professional life whenever I want just to be home with him.

But today is different.

There is no lounging around the house or getting our fill of one another. That isn't how we are. We made love a couple more times last night, once in the shower, and the other in our bed before we finally found sleep in one another's arms.

We were up before the sun, had a lunch and our camel packs ready to go, and watched as Trigger loaded into the truck for our day trip into the mountains.

Fishing or even taking in the wildlife weren't our focus. It is a hike to our spot. The rocky ravine decorated with pine trees and small spots of grass that overlook the stream below is our purpose today. Since he got his license, Daxon has brought us up here at least once a year just to sit and enjoy one another. Sometimes we see animals below going to water to drink, and on one rare occasion, we watched a bear chase some elk.

Not only are our names carved into a tree we have always found ourselves under, but the stone under us. It may seem like a regular spot on the mountain that you have to hike to, but to us, it's our place.

The hike itself doesn't take us long. Daxon found it one hunting season and started bringing me here the following summer.

Love, Mercy

"How long do you think I'll have you for?" Putting my camel pack down, I stare out at the scenery before us. It takes my breath away every time. I typically have an aversion to heights, but knowing that I'm here with Daxon, I know I have nothing to worry about.

And just as he knew my stomach was beginning to pitch from how far up we are, Daxon's arms wrap around my middle, and he was pulling me back into his strong chest.

"You know that answer." His chin rests on my shoulder as he bends down closer to me. "We can only live in the moment for now."

Sighing, my hands find their way to his arms. "I know, but I would like to think of the future."

"I've been putting some thought into that myself." His statement pierces my chest, but this time, it contains trace amounts of excitement.

"Oh?"

"I'm not sure when I will hang up my gear, but I may go to school. I don't know where to begin with what I want to do."

"I can see you becoming a personal trainer, maybe a furniture designer, you make great things out of trees, or even a high school gym teacher."

"I'm not *that* good around kids, Mercy."

He isn't fooling me. He's wonderful around kids. Now teenagers, on the other hand, are a different story. As if the simple word *kids* has the power to conjure something in front of me, my head begins to think of children. I'm settled enough in my career that a kid or two would be welcomed, but I'm not sure he's there yet. I know he wouldn't want to miss a moment of any of their lives, and I'm certain he isn't ready to retire yet.

"What's wrong, babe?"

"Hmm?"

"You locked up as if I'm ready to push you over the edge." He chuckles, turning me so he can get a better read on me. "What's going through your mind?"

And being who I am, I don't keep anything from him. I think that's why we have worked as well as we do have. One hundred percent honesty at all times. The only exception is his job and good surprises.

Love, Mercy

"I was thinking about kids." There isn't even a flinch at the word. His concerned gaze softens and if it were possible, it intensifies in warmth.

"I think about that all the time when I'm gone."

"You do?"

"Of course. Why wouldn't I want a little girl who looks just like her mom or a little boy who will be just as protective of you as I am?"

"But the military ..."

"And then I think about how if I were gone, I wouldn't get to see them grow like you do and wouldn't get to know them like I want to." His warmth still shines through even with the sadness edging in.

"Would you retire if kids came into the picture then?" I pause for half a heartbeat before I add. "I don't want to take you away from your passion or anything, but–"

"Mercy, babe, relax." He doesn't chuckle when he lifts my chin so I'm looking at him once more. He pulls us over to our tree and drops to the ground before settling me onto his lap. The wind is strong today, and with the lack of cover, it cuts past my sweaty back.

"You mean the world to me, Mercy, and so will any children we have, but I'm not ready to give up my career in the military. I'm good at what I do, and yes, it does keep me from you, but you are the most understanding and loving woman I could ever ask for."

"Because I know what it means to you."

"Because I live not just my dream but yours as well. I love you so much."

"It's not hard to wait for you. I'd even wait for you at the pearly gates if I go before you. There is no way I would want to walk through without you by my side."

"I couldn't agree with you more." He cuddles me closer, his hand pushing some of my loose hair behind my ears. "When the time comes for *kids,* we will have a serious talk about it because we are a team, and there is nothing one doesn't do without the other, okay?"

"Okay." When I nod, my face feels squished under his hands.

Love, Mercy

"Good. Now, kiss me, gorgeous. I need my wife right now."

Chapter Six

Mercy,

I went for a quick run, so if you wake before I get home, you have my words.

I love you. This weekend was beyond anything I could hope for. I know you are sad you have to go back to work today, but know that I will be here waiting when you get home this evening.

I may come steal you away for lunch, but that depends on what our dads have planned for our day. Pray they don't blow me up with their newest cannon. It would suck to get through all those tours of the middle east only to be maimed at home.

Have a wonderful day at work.

Love,

Daxon

ROLLING OVER TO FIND the scribbled note on Daxon's cooled pillow was not what I was hoping to find. I was slightly disappointed I couldn't cuddle with my husband.

Love, Mercy

I should have known that Daxon wouldn't be able to settle in completely. I was lucky enough to wake up next to him or making me breakfast for the past couple of mornings. He is a fine-tuned machine who has a set internal schedule that doesn't stop for anyone. On occasion, I would get up and go for a jog with him, but I've grown lazy in his absence. At least with joining his morning work outs. I've been saving all that for the evenings after work to fill the void.

Pulling the note to my chest, I roll until my face is in his pillow, and I can inhale his scent. It had begun to fade from the house a while ago. I relish in having it back where it belongs.

Once Daxon's unique fragrance floods my body, I get up and begin to go through the motions of getting ready. The house is quieter than normal, and when I get to the kitchen, I discover why. Daxon took Trigger with him.

I'm sure Trigger is loving the run.

With coffee in my mug, I turn and find my breakfast waiting for me under a cover. The plate is nestled next to the flowers he brought me Thursday, and my heart skips. Not only did he get up early to go for a run, but he made time to put breakfast together for me.

Lifting the cover, I discover a waffle, scrambled egg, and two strips of crispy bacon.

It doesn't take me long to polish off my breakfast, and then I'm getting ready. I don't particularly care to go to work, but I force myself into a pair of slacks, pale blue blouse, and black pumps. My honey blond hair is left to tumble down my back, my makeup is light, and I am out the door before I get a chance to see Daxon.

Using my butt to open the employee entrance, I back into the building and then turn to make my way to my office. For such a small town Centennial is, we are already busy this morning if the phones ringing and the tapping of fingers on keyboards is any indication.

When I turn on the light to my office, I'm relieved not to see a mountain of work on my desk. While my computer boots up, I turn on my little radio and catch the tail end of one of Jilly Meadows' songs before the host comes back on with the local morning news.

And that is how I lose myself for the next several hours. I check emails, go over paperwork, call back anyone who has left me a message, and end up staring at my computer screen.

Love, Mercy

It doesn't seem like much, but it eats away at my morning. The next thing I know, my coffee is long gone, my water bottle needs refill, I need a bathroom break, and Gretchen, our receptionist, is standing in my doorway wearing a huge smile.

"Yes?" I find this strange because normally she just calls an office if she has something for one of us.

"You have a special delivery." Her smile turns wicked as she swings out of the door to make way for whatever is being delivered to me. Unless I order lunch, I rarely get something not work-related delivered to me here.

"Oh?" Standing, I start to make my way around my desk when the delivery turns into a single person with a brown paper bag. Carried on two strong legs, familiar ones at that, I drag my gaze up those powerful columns to the tapered waist, the broad chest, toned arms and shoulders, and settle on the face I love more than any other.

"They didn't blow me up." Daxon spreads his arms to show off his completely intact body. And as much as I love taking it in, my stomach grumbles when the scent of something delicious and loaded with carbs finds its way to my nose.

"Please tell me that's a club bagel," I practically attack my man, pulling him into my office while he laughs.

"I see how it is. You only want me to bring you food."

"And other things, but I don't think doing that is wise here."

"Oh, but the fun we could have." His front presses into my back, and he thrusts the tiniest bit against my backside. Not enough for Gretchen, who I'm positive is eye-fucking my husband, to see but enough to make my breath hitch.

"Maybe … someday," I tease. "After hours and before the janitors come in." I blow him a kiss as I take my seat once more. "Now, what did you bring me?"

"Thanks, Gretchen." He addresses the woman frozen in the doorway, watching us before he closes the door and falls into one of my client seats. "Our favorites." Pulling out three wrapped bagels, I see one is marked for me, leaving the other two for him. "I was doing some thinking while I watched our dads attempt to look professional with primitive weapons."

Love, Mercy

"And what did you come up with?" My mouth is watering for this sandwich as much as it does for the man sitting across from me.

"Over the weekend and even today, I feel like I'm missing out on so much life." This causes me to pause, suspending the bagel sandwich in mid-air. "As much as I love what I do, I love you and my life here more."

Oh, my God, is he saying what I think he is?

"One more tour and I'm done, Mercy." Our gazes are locked when he states this. I'm going to melt. As much as I don't want to see him give up on what he loves to do, I'm thrilled at the prospect having him home more. "I don't know what exactly I want to do yet, but I've got time to figure it out."

"Are you sure?" I stutter.

"Absolutely." There isn't an ounce of hesitation as he answers me. "I want to be home with you now. I've given the military my time, and I've enjoyed it, but I'm ready to have a life here again."

There are no words to describe how much this means to me. I have never had an issue being a supportive military wife. I'm there to see him off on his tours, proud of him, and when I know he is coming home, I'm there to greet him. I love his patriotism; it helps boost my own.

Putting my lunch down, I get up and rush over to him, where I send us falling back into the wall with my impact, and I kiss him.

Chapter Seven

MY LIMP ARMS ARE lifted over my head, pulling me slowly from the slumber and warm spot in the bed.

Something smooth and soft slides around one wrist and then the other before they are pulled tightly.

Squeezing my eyes, I slowly begin to open them. The early morning light filters through the crack in the blinds, casting a ray into the room and acting as a spotlight as I look down to find my naked body uncovered, and Daxon standing on his knees between my parted legs.

"Good morning." The bed shifts as he comes down, bracing his strong arms on either side of me, and kisses me sweetly. Bad breath and all.

"Morning." I push back, trying to keep my nasty breath from hitting him in the face. It's bad enough that I have to taste it. "What are you up to?"

Against my better judgment, I have fallen into a routine with him. He has been home for nearly three months, and we have found a steady pace around here. While I work, Daxon hangs out with our retired dads or tries to figure out what he is going to do with his life once he is out. I teased that he could become a sheriff's deputy like our friend Duke Michaels and even though he said he wasn't interested in law enforcement, I know he's been by the station to talk to him.

Thank you, Patience.

I also mentioned he could work with our other friend, Holt Preston, as a bouncer over at his family's bar. That wasn't enticing enough for him either, but as he said, he has time to figure it out.

"Giving my beautiful wife some lovin' and a present." My nipples ache for his touch as each breath causes them to brush against his heated chest.

"Oh?" The single word turns into a moan. Sliding down my body, Daxon comes to a halt at my chest and wraps his tongue around one nipple before slipping it into his mouth. The overpowering need to thread my fingers into his hair that has grown a little has me pulling only to come up short when my arms don't move.

Love, Mercy

"Daxon." I mewl as he tortures my right nipple, frees it, and then captures the left with the same hunger. My body writhes under him. His massive body between my legs prevents me from rubbing my thighs together. My pussy aches for him. I'm wet and ready for him.

I love how he knows my body so well that he can bring me pleasure with a single touch.

"I love how you taste, Mercy," he murmurs against my sensitive flesh. Trailing down, he stops to dip his tongue into my navel. The first time he did it, it made me squirm with discomfort, but I've grown to love everything he does to me.

His tongue doesn't return to his mouth the lower he goes. The tip of his wicked tongue passes over my lower stomach, the top of my mound, and then effortlessly slips between my pussy lips.

"Fuck, you're soaked." His growl cause quivers to roll up my body. "Always so ready for me." He attacks me as though I'm his breakfast. His hunger is rough and delicious. I continue to writhe on the bed, my arms straining with the need to touch him. Aside from causing my shoulder to tense, it increases the sensations he is giving to me.

Higher and higher, I reach ever closer to the precipice. I'm so close to the edge of coming by his mouth alone, and then his delicious torture is gone. Eyes snapping open, I look up to find Daxon bracing himself over me once more. The wickedness in his grin and the mirth in his gaze quicken my pulse. My need for the release he was about to give me isn't going anywhere.

I'm just fine with the lack of foreplay. I don't need it with him. All he has to do is give me that look, the one he is giving me now, and I'm ready for him to consume me, to get lost in me as I do the same with him.

Reaching between us, he helps guide his velvety steel length into my body. I stretch and swallow him as if I were made to fit only him. My mouth parts. He takes it as an invitation to advance his assault on my body, mind, and soul.

Settled within me, Daxon pauses. Not a movement, not even a kiss occurs in the seconds that pass as we just take in the feel of one another. He rolls his hips, pulling out, and sharply pushes back into me with a force that I would only be comfortable with from him, especially with my hands bound.

Love, Mercy

Each time he begins to pull out of me, his shaft rubs against my G-spot and clit before he slams back into me. The mixture of sweet and punishing is wonderful.

His lips trial to my neck, where he places kisses. Even though I know he wants to mark me as his, he won't. We are adults, and I don't own anything that would cover it up. I too want to leave my mark on him, but seeing as my wrists are tied and my arms are pulled over my head, I won't be doing anything of the sort right now.

Once more, my body begins to climb higher up the mountain of love he is erecting with each thrust. I'm lost in pleasure, wild with desire, and so consumed that I begin to lose my grip on reality until I am screaming, and my entire body is pulled so tight that I'm sure not even Daxon can move.

The haze of euphoria begins to clear only for pleasure to take hold of me once more. My eyes feel as if they were on fire as I open and look up at him. The concentration he has is awe-inspiring, but the tightness in his jaw is all I need to know that he barely has a hold on his control.

"Please, Daxon," I pant. "Let go."

And like that, he does. The man showcases so much strength and restraint in his life but the power of my words are just what he needs to let go.

Thrust after rapid thrust, Daxon takes my body with him once more as our releases interweave, and we both fall apart.

Our breathing is crazed, our chests rising and falling with deep breaths, and I'm thankful he doesn't collapse on top of me as he does from time to time. I get to stare up at him, his eyes closed but I know his gaze will be on me the moment they open.

"I love you so much." My voice is cracked and dry. I need water, but I need this closeness more.

"I love you, too, babe." Not opening his eyes, he leans down to kiss me sweetly, and before he can pull himself free of me, he reaches up and frees my arms.

Flexing my fingers, I roll my wrists and then my shoulders. The movement causes something to poke me between my breasts as they too move.

"What the …?" Trailing off, I fumble with my slightly numb fingers as they reach my chest, and it is then that I notice I'm wearing something. "Daxon?" Still not leaving my body, he moves us until I'm sitting on his lap, his arms caging me in close to him.

"Surprise." Kissing my shoulder, I lift the necklace as he watches me closely. Frowning, I look at the half dollar-sized pendant. It is light and delicate for its size. I don't know what it is. It somewhat resembles a s–

"It's supposed to be the Northern Star." If I couldn't love this man more, he reads my musing. "You are my Northern Star, Mercy. No matter where in the world I am to go or what may happen, my compass will always point to you."

Tears burn my eyes at the meaning behind this necklace.

"I'll never take it off then." Placing it gently back against my chest, I tilt my head to kiss him only to have the sound of his phone invade our bubble.

Daxon,

While you were showering, I decided to subject you to my horrible handwriting. I know you aren't going to find this until you get to where you will be settled enough to unpack, and that's how I plan this.

I love you. I love everything about you and the life you have given me. I can't wait until you can be back in my arms for good. Every time I feel like I need you a little closer, I'm going to hold onto the beautiful necklace you gave me. I have a feeling that will be often.

Stay safe and know that I will be here waiting for you when you return. I can't wait to see what our future will look like. I have so much more to say, but I'm going to keep this short and sweet because I don't think you want to carry a book around. I know you aren't going to let this go anywhere without you.

Stay safe, my soldier.

Love, Mercy

Chapter Eight

LIKE EVERY TIME HE'S HOME, the visits are too short, but this time, he was home a little longer.

I drove him to Great Falls to catch his flight to who knows where he is to check in with his superiors. His goodbyes to our family were quick and painless, but as I walked into the airport with him, our goodbye was not the same.

I clung to him, my tears soaking into his shirt as I sobbed. I didn't want that to be the impression I left, but it was nearly impossible to keep my eyes dry. Our goodbyes are never easy, especially when I want to go with him.

As his flight was called, Daxon took a step back, breaking our connection to hold me at arm's length. *"I promise you, Mercy. I will get a hold of you as soon as I can. I don't know what I'm going in to, but know I'm thinking of you."*

With one last searing kiss, I was left behind. My hand fisted around the necklace as he turned around and walked away. I fought to keep my tears at bay, so my sight of him was unobstructed until he was no longer visible.

I didn't leave until his plane was in the air. While I watched it climb higher into the late afternoon sky, I sent up a prayer that he would return to me soon and safely. God knows where this assignment will lead him, but I need to have faith in the almighty.

When I got into my car, I took in his presence that still lingered around me. It made it bearable to get back on the highway to head home. Music helped to a point, but every song that came on still felt like a reminder of him.

Normally, I'm not a fan of making this trip on my own, but luckily the nice weather means I don't have to worry about the wind keeping me from getting home quickly.

By the time I reach the outskirts of Centennial, it's dinnertime, and I'm thankful I don't have to go back to my house and feel the loneliness just yet.

Instead of getting off at the exit leading to my house, I get off on the next one and head to my parents' home. It has become customary to have a family dinner the night Daxon leaves because our moms both understand having an empty home. My dad didn't retire until the mid-nineties so my mom is all too accustomed to what I'm going through.

Daxon's parents are already there by the time I pull up and make my way into my childhood home. Sometimes, my friends join us, but tonight, I wanted just the family.

I'm mopey as I make my way to the dining room, and the freely floating laughter warms me up. Around the table my dad and I made when I was in junior high sits my family. The people who have been there for me through every deployment and helped raise my spirits when I couldn't live out my dream.

"You made it back quicker than we thought." My dad's booming voice does little to pull me from my sadness. He gets out of his chair and quickly wraps me in his embrace while telling my mom she could put the finishing touches on dinner now that I've arrived. "Hey, trooper."

"Hey, Dad." His burly chest muffles my voice, but it feels good to be wrapped in a hug.

Kissing the top of my head, he whispers, "Everything is going to be okay."

Nodding is all I can do before I free myself and make my trip around the table to hug everyone before I can take my seat.

They know better than to try to cheer me up. The first week is usually the hardest for me, but I'll be okay after that.

The conversation continues around me even as dinner is served, and I mope. My food, my favorite meal of fried chicken and mashed potatoes, is pushed around my plate.

I don't pay attention to what people are saying around me. All I can think about is where Daxon is now, and what he has to do before he can return to me for good.

Everything is going to be okay.

He's a capable man; strong and resourceful. This mission will be just like the others, and then he will be here to help me with my committees and our life.

"Mercy?" My dad's concerned voice pulls me from my musings. Dragging my gaze up, I find four sets of eyes locked on me.

"Hmm?"

"I told you it wouldn't last." His smile is warm. "He'll retire. Maybe not today, but someday soon."

Love, Mercy

I can't bring myself to tell them he already has plans to do so. I'm not given the chance to reply because my dad says the one thing that puts a smile on my face.

"And then you two can get to work on giving us grandchildren."

Chapter Nine

AA HARD AS IT IS TO BELIEVE, time has flown by since Daxon left. I have yet to hear from him but that's not uncommon. His job takes him directly from home and places him in some of the hardest to reach places on Earth. Doing what he does, I've grown accustomed to only hearing from him periodically.

This time is no different.

A month has gone by, and I've found myself getting back to my normal. The company I work for has been busy partnering up with another company in Sheridan, Wyoming. They have had an influx of clients and since it is our sister company, we have been focusing on things from the Powder River area. Sometimes, I'm at the office long after the janitors come and go since I have to wait on emails to come up from the other office.

And because of that, I've become an early morning runner just to make sure I get some sort of a work out in. Trigger absolutely loves getting out first thing in the morning because he rules the paths we run. There is rarely another dog or runner out at the same time as us.

Love, Mercy

In a way, it makes me feel even closer to Daxon. As if I could get any closer. Figuratively speaking, my husband and I are closer than close. The time and distance between us don't make a difference whatsoever. Each time I see his handsome face feels like he was there the day before.

This time around, it's a little easier to handle the silence that greets me after I've settled Trigger down at home because I know he won't be going anywhere in the world after this trip without me.

Angie and I have spent time with Patience at her bakery, where I've indulged in way too many carbs. They have helped me keep my mind off the worry.

We have had a few girls' nights out both at the Grizzly and at one of our homes for movies. I'm thankful for the people in my life.

Something in the back of my skull buzzes as I step into the house. I'm late, and I'm bracing myself for Trigger's attack because I'm sure he is hungry. Once my heels are off, and my purse is placed in my bedroom, I make my way to the kitchen find him staring up at me while lying next to his food bowl.

"Hey, buddy. Sorry I'm late." Before I can even think of my own insatiable hunger, I go to the pantry and fill up his bowl and then check his water. I swear I've constantly been hungry for the past two weeks.

My grumbling stomach keeps me from going to the bathroom to shower and change into something less restricting. I'm not sure how to take it because, aside from the possibility of too many baked goods from Patience, there is only one other reason my clothing could be starting to feel tight. As professionally as I dress for my job, I make it a point only to buy things I know will be comfortable.

Going to the fridge, I pull out the leftover chicken, bacon, and artichoke pizza I made myself two nights ago and popped a couple of pieces in the microwave, then start to steam some vegetables. While all of that is being done, the all-consuming need for orange juice takes hold of me, so I open the fridge again to grab the jug and drink directly from it.

"Oh, that feels good."

Once my meal is made, and Trigger is in the backyard running around before I lock up for the night, I set up shop at my desktop and pull up my emails. Every night I come home and do this to see if Daxon has sent me anything. And like every time, my heart swells with hope only to plummet when.

Falling back in my seat, I start to eat. Mindlessly, I'm staring at the unchanging screen while I shovel food down my throat. I feel so famished for just having had a protein bar this afternoon. A slice of pizza is hanging out of my mouth when Skype pops up, indicating that I have an incoming video call.

Swallowing the barely chewed piece of food, I lean up to accept it when I see Daxon's name. The video may be touch and go, but I keep this service just to be able to see his face when we can talk. Accepting the call, it takes a minute for the screen to clear up and the lag to set in on his smiling face.

"Hey, babe."

"Hi." I'm giddy, squirming in my seat at the sight of him. "How are you?"

He sighs, and I know it isn't good. "Could be better." The lag acts like it takes snap shots of him as he collapses back in his seat. "Thank you for the letter. You were right. I'm carrying it right here." He pats his breast pocket.

"You're welcome. What's going on?" I know he can't tell me much, but I can ask and see.

"We just got our next assignment." There is another sigh. "I don't know when I'll be coming home after this, Mercy. We are going in deep, and it's going to be ugly, but it needs to be done." He isn't thrilled about this, but it's all part of the job. "I don't know when I'll be able to talk to you again, and even now, our time is limited." He looks away as if to check something.

"It's okay. I'll take whatever I can get." I hope my soft smile reassures him. "I know you'll be okay and the next thing you know, you'll be coming home to me."

"God, I wish I could come home now, but this needs to be done." Repeating his words, he seems as if he's trying to convince himself more than me.

"I'll pray." It takes everything in me to keep my voice from fading to a whisper so he can hear me.

"I know, babe." He leans forward again. He looks cramped in a tiny room. "I'll be home soon." He smiles at me and I relax for a second. "I love you."

"I love you, too." Kissing my hand, I put my fingers up, and he repeats the same.

"Behave, Mercy."

Love, Mercy

"I'll do my best." The call then disconnects. It was far too short, but at least it was something. Whatever he has going on has him worried and, in turn, has concern fluttering in my chest.

As I pull myself back together, I go through the motions of getting ready for bed. Trigger settled in his bed next to mine when I locked up, and I change into one of Daxon's shirt before settling into bed.

Slumber doesn't come easy, and when I do finally fall asleep, I toss and turn. Sweat starts to make me itchy and uncomfortable. Suddenly, I'm shooting upright in bed. Looking over at the clock it's 3:00 a.m. My heart is racing, and my stomach is knotting and rolling uncomfortably. The next thing I know, I'm rushing to the bathroom and throwing up everything left in my stomach.

Chapter Ten

MY MIND WON'T ALLOW me to settle, so I don't bother going back to bed once I'm done puking my guts out. I'm not even comfortable resting my cheek against the closed lid of the toilet. The heat radiating off my body causes the cool porcelain to sting on contact.

Trigger comes in and cuddles near my bare legs. I'm positive he is doing his best to comfort me. His warm, soft body feels nice next to me, but I'm still restless. I don't know how long I sit there, wondering if I'm going to get sick again, but eventually, my legs protest my position and I force myself onto wobbly legs.

The moonlight reaching through the curtains glistens across my upheaved bed as I walk by with a longing look. As much as I want to crawl back under the covers and clutch Daxon's pillow to me, I can't bring myself to settle down enough.

Something isn't sitting right in my stomach.

Mindlessly, I make my way to the living room and turn on my computer once more. There is no way I'm going to be able to reach Daxon, wherever he is. I don't know who else to get a hold of at this time of night, so I do the only thing I can.

I fire up my email and write to him.

Daxon,

It's only been a few hours since we talked, and I have to admit, I'm worried. I woke up with a start, threw up, and now I can't get back to sleep. You know that I don't normally have a sense of something foreboding or anything, but something is off. I don't know if it has to do with this mission you are going on or what, but I'm feeling uneasy.

I don't want to worry you about anything, but I don't know who else to turn to right now. I'm praying whatever is going on with me has nothing to do with you. If you get this before you have to go out, know that I love you more than anything in existence, and I'm praying for your safe and quick return to me.

I'm going to be okay, and so are you. I guess I just needed to find something to settle me and talking to you, or writing, in this case, is the only thing that helps.

Be safe.

Love, Mercy

Pushing send, I back away from the screen and feel lost. I don't know what to do now. Going back to sleep isn't going to work for me, so I turn on some music, then return to my room to put on a pair of socks. I have to find something, anything to help me settle.

I end up cleaning the entire house. The cabinets, the fridge, the bookcase, and the entertainment center—nothing was safe from my need to clean. I spend hours going from room to room, singing along to the songs that come on, and do what I can to keep my mind off things.

When the sun starts to peek over the horizon, fatigue grabs me. Going into the kitchen, I make myself toast, eggs, and down more orange juice after shutting off the coffee pot before it can start to brew. I don't think I can stomach the bitter fluid this morning.

It's eight by the time I settle back between the sheets. I checked my email while I ate and had nothing from Daxon. A yawn rattles through me as I stare down at my phone only to rip the sheets off me so I can rush back to the bathroom to bring my breakfast back up.

I'm burning up, my forehead is overheated, and my stomach doesn't settle even as I stagger back to the bedroom.

Love, Mercy

Pulling up my contacts, I call the office to let them know I need to take a sick day. When I'm reassured that everything will be handled and told to rest and get better, I pull the covers over my head and try to get some shut-eye.

I fall into a dreamless sleep. No dreams or nightmares, which I'm okay with. I'm sure I sleep for a few hours before my bed shifting pulls me from it.

Groggily, I roll to my back and force my eyes to open, finding not only my mom sitting at the foot of my bed but Daxon's as well.

"Mom? Tina?" Yawning, I stretch and slowly sit up. "What are you two doing here?"

"We saw your car was still here."

"And knew you wouldn't walk to work." It's kind of freaky how they can explain something as if they have a hive mind.

"So, we thought we would come to check on you." Tina squeezes my foot while my mom crawls up the bed to cradle me to her.

"What's going on, Mercy?"

I've never been one to keep things to myself for the most part. If something is bothering me, I tell someone. Usually, that person is Daxon, but our moms are a close second and third.

I tell them about the unease and finish with how I threw up twice now. Once I'm done, they are speechless, and regarding one another with something I can only compare to being overjoyed.

"What?" Pulling my sheet up my chest like a forcefield, my mom only nods, and then Tina is gone. The front door slams moments after she vacates my room. "Mom?"

"When was your last period, Mercy?"

My eyes widen as realization slams into me. "Umm …" I can't answer her.

"Mercy, breathe." Mom's hand finds its way to my back, where she begins to rub. "It's going to be okay," she murmurs in the tone only a loving mother can have.

Daxon and I have never used protection. After we got married, we decided to leave having kids up to fate. He isn't here, though. I can't go through all of this without him. Or can I?

Love, Mercy

No, I don't want him to miss anything. The test, the first appointment, the first kick, all of it. I don't know when he's going to be home. I'm so lost in my thoughts that I don't notice Tina is back and placing a box she pulled from a plastic bag on my lap.

Two tests, two chances to find out if what they are thinking and what I know deep down is true.

"Come on, Mercy." Mom is off the bed and coaxing me to do the same. She holds onto me as I make my way to the bathroom and then helps me open the tests before reading the instructions and leaving me to do what needs to be done.

I don't like calling it a scare because we never saw it as one, but we thought at the beginning of our marriage that I could be pregnant, so I know what to do. It turned out I was just late, which was something rare for me, and we never ended up telling anyone. But now, I have a feeling everything is different.

Pulling down my panties, I do as the box instructs, and then we wait. Sitting back down on the bed, I am flanked by both women. Each grabs a hand as we wait for the timer to go off. Trigger must sense something is off because he comes in and rests his head on my lap.

I feel like I'm floating when I go back in to collect the test.

Brooke May

The very positive test.

Daxon,

I know, I'm emailing you more than normal, but life just changed for us. Our moms helped me figure out why I was feeling so off.

Daxon, I'm pregnant. We are going to be parents, so you better make sure you do the very best job you can and get home to me soon because I don't want to go through this pregnancy without you. We are going to have a baby soon, and I hope he looks like you.

Don't ask me; I just have a feeling this baby is a boy. One who will be just as handsome as his dad, strong and protective like him too.

I can't wait to have you by my side at doctor's appointments and when this baby comes into this world.

Come home to me soon.

Love, Mercy

Chapter Eleven

"SOMETHING'S WRONG." Wringing my hands around the magazine I absentmindedly picked up after I checked in, I can't keep the worry from consuming me.

"Everything is going to be just fine, sweetheart." Mom's warm hand covers my trembling knee, but it does nothing to calm my nerves. "Once you see the baby on the ultrasound, you'll see."

"That's not what I'm worried about, Mom." I'm doing everything in my power to keep control of the wavering in my voice. There is so much more going through my mind that what should be in the forefront, my pregnancy, isn't.

After I took the test and emailed Daxon, I went into autopilot. Mom called and set up my appointment for me. They had to pull me out of my funk so I could figure out when my last period was so they could tell the doctor's office how far along I might be.

That was two weeks ago, and I haven't heard from Daxon. Typically, it isn't an issue. We sometimes go a couple of months between talking or seeing each other, but something is off this time. Maybe it is just my own urgency to tell him our news, but my stomach curdles when I try to convince myself that is it.

"What's going on, honey?" Tina's hand comes to rest on my other knee. Honestly, if I could find the humor in this, it would be laughable at having them on either side me because I'm usually completely okay doing things on my own. But I'm grateful they are here with me. Aside from going through the motions at work and making sure I am taking care of myself, my life has been nonexistent outside of any of that.

They picked me up and delivered me here.

When I take a shuddering breath, my entire body trembles as I blow it out. "I'm worried about Daxon." Admitting that is easy, but it doesn't take away the anxiety.

"Sweetie." Mom wraps an arm around me, pulling me to her side. "He's okay. You know what his job entails, but he has always takes his safety to a height that I haven't seen anyone else take it before. Not even your dad."

"He is always keeping a watchful eye and taking precautions to get back home to us and to you," Tina adds in.

"You'll hear from him before you know it, and all this worry will fade away. Then you'll be able to enjoy this."

Their words comfort me. Not completely, it still feels as though a knife is about to pierce my heart, but I can relax a little. Hopefully, my blood pressure won't be through the roof.

"Mercy Logan?"

Each of us looks up to the nurse standing in the doorway. Another shuddering breath is pulled in as I stand, and the supportive women on either side of me join me. My blood pressure was perfect, and my weight is normal, even though I've lost a few pounds. Getting sick every time you eat will do that. I managed *not* to pee all over my hand while leaving my urine sample. Then I'm escorted into a room where I'm told to change into the gown laid out on the exam table and that the doctor will be in shortly.

Mom and Tina stay with me. They take the two available seats in the small room while I climb onto the exam table, and we wait. My nerves are on edge that the knock on the door has me jumping.

"Good morning, Mrs. Logan. I'm Dr. Wagner." A kind-looking man steps in with a nurse following him. Of course, I know who he is. He delivered Patience and Duke's baby two months ago and happens to be the only OB/GYN in town.

"Hi." My voice is faint.

"I believe a congratulations is in order." His smile is welcoming, but I'm still unable to relax. From the pelvic exam and taking measurements, I'm struggling to breathe. "Everything looks good. Your urine sample confirmed that you are indeed pregnant." He snaps the gloves off at the same time the nurse dims the lights. "Now, shall we see your baby and see how far along you are?"

"O-Okay," I stammer. I'm not sure what to expect, but when he inserts the probing ultrasound in me after putting new gloves on, I'm shocked at how cold it is.

"Sorry about that. We've been meaning to update these with the built-in warmers." And then silence. Aside from the tapping of the computer keys as he makes notes, no one says a word. Mom and Tina are on my left side while the nurse stands behind Dr. Wagner. "And there we have it." Turning my head on the paper-covered pillow, I look at the screen where he is pointing and frown.

"Wh-what?"

"That's your baby, sweetie." Mom leans forward to whisper. And sure enough, I see movement.

"Is that ... its heart?"

"Yes." He taps another key, and then there is a whooshing sound. We listen for a moment before he speaks again. "And by the sounds of it, a good, strong heart."

Tears burn my eyes. I'm overjoyed while at the same time I'm sad that Daxon is missing this.

"You're measuring around six weeks." I hear a printer, and then the probe is gone, and so is my baby. "We will set up your appointments once we finish here, and you can take some of these." He hands me a couple of ultrasound pictures and I'm free to go once I get changed.

I'm in another universe as I'm guided out. My mind reels with getting these ultrasounds scanned and sent to Daxon. But I don't need to wait for that. While my mom and Tina take me home, I do my best to take pictures of them with my phone and quickly shoot off an email. I keep it brief, just telling him the baby's heart rate, when my due date should be, and that I love him.

Once I send it, I feel a little better.

Daxon,

I know that its likely you won't read this, but I need to write. In fact, I'm saying all of this out loud as I type. I just received the news. Well, not just received; it's been a few hours and a couple of boxes of tissues, but I finally pulled myself together enough to write these words.

I love you. To the deepest depths on our planet to throughout the universe, I love you.

I've been told that your mission went bad, and the likelihood of you coming home to me isn't great, but I don't believe any of that. I know you'll find your way back to me someway, somehow, Daxon. I know it might sound foolish or something along those lines, but I truly believe it; no matter what others say, you will be home.

I emailed you earlier today with our news. I feel like I need to say it again on for the off chance you manage to get back to somewhere you can check this. I'm pregnant. You are going to be a father, so you need to hurry home because I don't want to do this without you.

I can't say it enough. I love you, Daxon. Please come home to me.

Brooke May

Love, Mercy

Daxon,

We are having a girl!

Months have come and gone with no word from you, but my hope isn't going anywhere. Even if they closed down your email, and gets a returned, I'm still writing to you.

As you know from my last letter, morning sickness was taking its toll on me. It's gotten better after I passed the twelve-week mark, but some of it lingers if I'm around certain foods or smells. Our moms were by my side at the ultrasound. It was crazy because I could clearly make out her face.

As much as I was hoping for a little boy who looked just like you, I'm happy our baby is doing well and growing quickly. She does look like you, though. At least I think she does. The ultrasound was amazing even though it was still a little difficult to make out other parts of her.

I love her just as much as I love you.

Please, Daxon. Come home.

Love, Mercy

Daxon,

She's here!

A week late, Layla made her entrance to the world. She's the most beautiful person I have ever seen, babe. She has your nose and skin tone, but she has my eyes and hair. To me, she is the perfect combination of both of us. She is currently sleeping next to me in her bed, and I'm exhausted, but I needed to tell you. I'm sure when we get home, I won't be getting much rest until I have her on a sleep schedule.

I wish you were here.

Please, come home safely.

Love, Mercy

Daxon,

I have done my best to keep up with every milestone that Layla has had over the past few months, and I'm hoping I haven't missed a single one to share with you.

I haven't received an undeliverable notice yet for any of my emails, so here I am, writing to you while Layla is going crazy in her bouncer. She has such strong little legs.

I am still holding on to hope that you are with us and will be coming home soon. I don't know how to explain it when someone attempts to talk to me about you. They feel that if you were still alive, you would have found your way home by now, but something deep in my soul tells me you are fighting your hardest to return.

I wait for you every day.

Love, Mercy

Chapter Twelve

A year later

"WHAT THE ...?" Jolting upright in bed, I instantly grab my head as pain sears through it. I thought I would be used to waking like this by now. No matter how much time has passed, I still don't sleep well. It has nothing to do with the crazy toddler with wild blond hair who runs circles around me even on my best day and everything to do with the fact that I still miss her daddy.

Nightmares have plagued me since the day I was given the news.

I see Daxon's handsome face crying out to me as something horrible happens to him, and the pain of that day returns to me full force, waking me from even the deepest of slumber. I have done everything in my civilian power to find out information about my husband. No one will tell me anything except they tried for a long time to get to Daxon and his men before they finally had to give up. This was kept out of the news, and each family had to suffer in silence over their lost loved one.

Love, Mercy

I had to find a way to be strong and carry on, not for my own life but for the life I carried within me. Nightmares led to headaches, and headaches led to worry and anxiety that caused issues with my pregnancy. Sleep was too difficult to obtain.

But this morning seems different.

The bedroom is cool from the early November chill, and I think it is time to start turning up the heat. Getting out of bed, I hear the ear-piercing squeal coming from somewhere in the house and then the clicking of Trigger's claws on the hardwood.

"Momma!" I'm barely a foot out of my bedroom when Layla's chunky toddler legs bring her to me. My one-year-old hits me like a freightliner before I'm able to grab her.

"What, baby?"

Three months ago, I finally had to transform her crib into her toddler bed. She kept escaping, and I didn't want to risk her falling and hurting herself.

"Tigger!" Her little button nose wrinkles in disgust. She can't say Trigger, so he has become Tigger to her. We even dressed him up as the bouncing tiger for Halloween this year.

"Let's go see what he did." Inwardly, I groan as we make our way through the house until we find him by the back door next to a nice pile of vomit, waiting for me to clean it up. "Wonderful."

After putting Layla in her high chair, I lay some paper towels on top of the puke, then let Trigger outside. I turn on the radio and then gather the ingredients to start making our breakfast and I can't fight my smile as Layla begins to dance in her chair the best she can. She is the brightest light in my otherwise dull life. Nothing has ever been the same since Daxon's disappearance. I leave it at that. He disappeared because, to me, I can't bring myself to believe he is truly gone.

There is no grave marker because we didn't have a funeral for him. Even when others tried to convince me that we needed to so everyone who was in Daxon's life could move on, I couldn't do it. Thankfully, those people weren't the ones closest to him. Our family as well as our friends, agreed with my wishes. We honored Daxon for his service and sacrifice, but no one has gone against me with my belief that he might still be alive.

My soul still cries out for its other half, and deep down, there is a yearning that feels the echoes of something responding.

Love, Mercy

I don't tell anyone this because I don't want them to think I've gone crazy.

And I'm not.

Aside from our family and friends, everyone else around me thinks of me as a widow who is in denial. That might be so because it has been over a year, but the love Daxon and I shared isn't something I can move on from. It ran deep and powerful, and that isn't easy to forget or recover from.

And that's why I have donated more time to the committees that help veterans as well as active servicemen and women. Last year, I led the charge in putting together a parade for Veteran's Day. Our friend Chase carried a picture of Daxon for me in the parade.

This year, we're focusing on honoring everyone by setting up a procession that will begin with the only two World War II veterans left in our small town and ending with the active servicemen and women who are currently home.

I'm thrilled at the community involvement with this.

"Momma?" Placing her small bowl of oatmeal in front of her, I watch her little toddler legs swing madly under her small table.

"Yes, baby?" I place my bowl down and then go back to finish cooking my egg.

"Work?"

"Yes, that means you get to go play with Gramma and Mimi." Those two have always watched Layla for me after I had to return to work. They take turns every week with whose house they'll be at, but they love surrounding their granddaughter with hugs and kisses, and she enjoys playtime with them and the friends she's made through story time at the library.

"Yay!"

"Eat your breakfast, and we'll get ready to go." This morning is going to be a little different for me. I'll drop Layla off, then head to my meeting to finalize the parade, and then I'm off to work.

While I was pregnant, everyone told me that I would never be on time again once Layla was born. I proved them all wrong. We are always early, even on mornings like this when a wrench is thrown in.

Love, Mercy

That's just something I love to do. Proving people wrong makes me feel good because I can go against what they say and come out smelling like roses.

I get myself ready for the day after cleaning up and feeding Trigger, start the car, and finally get Layla ready for her day of fun with her grandmas.

We are out the door in thirty minutes with military precision, but not before Layla does her daily routine of stopping by the picture of Daxon in our living room and kissing him.

Chapter Thirteen

THE WONDERFUL THING ABOUT working for my company is the availability of an empty conference room in the mornings.

After dropping Layla off with her grandmas and having to pull her off me, I'm rushing into the building to make it to the meeting I'm supposed to be running.

I've never had issues with dropping her off before, but for some reason, this morning was different. It's Friday, so I played it off as her wanting to be closer to me. Since having her, I have cut back on work. I don't go into the office at all hours of the night and weekends to keep my mind busy. I spend all my extra time with her.

Exactly how it should be.

I'm just as ready for the weekend as she is. We'll be going on a hike tomorrow before helping with things for the parade on Sunday. It's amazing how much this has grown in recent years. Most businesses are even postponing their opening that morning until afterward. The high school is also excusing seniors to come down and help. I will have the senior cheerleaders marching alongside each generation with red, white, and blue pom-poms.

Taking a split second to compose my rushed self, I inhale and enter the boardroom we are using this morning. I can see Gretchen already set out the donuts I ordered and put the coffeepot out for any who would like some.

"Good morning, everyone. I'm so sorry to keep you." I don't give an excuse because most of them won't care.

Dropping into the seat close to the donuts, I smile at everyone around the table. This committee has grown as well. We went from a few older members of society to fifteen different people. There is one new face this year, my co-worker Marcus. But I'm certain the only reason he joined is to get to me.

The man is good looking, I'll give him that, but I'm *not* attracted to him. My heart still belongs to Daxon. Every other single woman in our building fawn over him, but I'm not one. I reasoned that he seems to think of me as a conquest or some sort of trophy to gain since I've turned him down. That's just the type of man he is, and that is not sexy.

He carries himself like some sort of god to women, and I'm the only one not feeding into it.

"No worries, Mercy." Marcus has somehow secured the seat closest to me. Leaning back in his chair, he presses the end of his pen to his grinning lips. "We were just going over each of our responsibilities."

"Thank you." I do everything I can to keep the bite from my response. I'm not the only one annoyed at his joining, especially since he just so happened to stumble into our first meeting a couple of months ago. After seeing me inside, he's invited himself to join.

Pulling out my notebook, I finally look up at everyone. Some are in business attire like Marcus and me while others are in regular clothing, and then there is our sheriff. We all blend for our veterans.

"Please, continue. I'll make my notes so everything is clear over the weekend, and we can cover anything that may have been overlooked before Monday morning."

For the next half hour, we discuss everything from how traffic will be detoured starting at seven to where refreshment stands will be available for people as well as space heaters just in case it's cold. I'm in charge of the high schoolers helping out.

Love, Mercy

All in all, everything goes perfectly, and we are all out of there in an orderly time.

Since I don't have to rush off across town, I take my time to help straighten up the conference room as the others leave. I'm saying my goodbyes and then humming to myself as I put the trash together for the janitors later when I turn around, and Marcus is right there.

He's in my space, and I don't care for it.

If I wasn't at work, but at the Grizzly, I wouldn't hesitate to put him in his place.

"Marcus." I nod to him before ducking and going back to collecting my things only to have him trailing behind me.

He's. Too. Damn. Close.

Biting down on my cheek, I don't even force a smile. To a man like Marcus, a smile is an open invitation to be even more forward.

"Thank you." I'm curt, and my tone brooks no argument as I skirt around him to head out to my office, leaving him holding the door open for me.

"What do you say you and me get a bite for lunch?" I don't stop because I know he would only slam into my back, and that would give him the opportunity to touch me.

"I'm sorry, Marcus, but I'm busy."

"That's what you always say." He groans. "Come on, one meal." He touches me. My body has never grown this rigid this quickly. Abruptly, I turn on my heels and shoot a glare up at him.

"Marcus, thank you for the multiple offers, but I am going to refuse you until you get the hint and leave me alone. There are plenty of other women you can ask, and they would gladly go out with you. I am not one of them."

Turning back around, I'm sure he won't follow me, but his words halt me.

"You know he's dead, right? You can't love a man who is no longer breathing, Mercy."

Fury, white-hot and ready to burst from me like I haven't felt in years, bubbles under the surface of my skin. Turning back around, I am about to rip him a new one when a voice booms in the hallway.

Love, Mercy

"Marcus, may I see you in my office, *please*?"

Marcus's eyes grow to the size of saucers at our boss's request. Wordlessly, Marcus turns around and heads to our boss's office while I look on to see him glaring and giving me a single nod before following the other man.

That nods says it all. He has my back, and I'm grateful.

Once more, I head to my office and don't stop until I'm falling into my chair and looking at the picture of Daxon next to my phone. And as relieved as I am about my boss stepping in, I can't help but wonder if there isn't some truth in Marcus's words.

Chapter Fourteen

AN EERIE SILENCE SURROUNDS me when I step into my mom's house. It's frigid and slightly haunting the deeper I get into the house.

Something is wrong. The hairs on the back of my neck are telling me that much.

"Mom?" I peek in the kitchen and find it empty. "Tina?" The backyard is also empty. "Layla?" As I pass the hallway to head to the living room, movement causes me to stop.

"Layla?" Shuffling out of my old room, she rubs her eyes and makes her way over to me.

"Momma." Using grabby hands, she sleepily asks me to pick her up. She doesn't have to ask me twice. Bending down, I pull her to me and bury my nose into her hair. I swear there is a lingering scent there that doesn't belong on her.

It's a smell that belongs to only one person.

Daxon.

Love, Mercy

Ice slices into my heart at the fading scent of my husband. How could she possibly smell like him or am I just day dreaming? Once we are standing upright, I take another deep breath but there is nothing. The ice remains in my heart as I carry her to the living room.

"Where are those grandmas of yours?" I murmur into her hair, still trying to find that scent, but it's gone. If it was really even there to begin with.

She mutters something I couldn't possibly understand as she cuddles deeper into my neck. Her little fingers find some of my hair, and she begins to twirl it.

"It's a little late for you to be napping. Looks like we are going to have to have a slumber party in our living room and watch movies tonight. How does that sound?"

She giggles in response.

"And maybe have pizza for dinner?"

"Piz!"

One more step and we are in the wide living room. The wall on the far side is nothing but windows and overlooks the vast backyard and the river that cuts through the bottom of my parents' property. Usually, my mom has already drawn the curtains for the evening, but not today.

Sniffles pull my attention away from the doe and fawn grazing on the browning grass and over to the couch where both women sit.

"Mom? Tina?" Worried about them, I hurry over and sit on the coffee table with Layla still in my arms. "What's wrong?"

I know something is definitely up because I'm not allowed to sit on the coffee table, not when I was Layla's age and certainly not now that I'm an adult.

Tina is a blubbering mess, reaching for more tissues while Mom blows her nose and blinks up at me.

"PMS."

"Together?" I'm baffled.

"We spend enough time together that our cycles have synced." Mom continues to dab at her eyes. I know this isn't an act. At least not the crying bit. That is very much real. The reasoning on the other hand, is what I'm not buying.

Love, Mercy

"I thought women don't have periods anymore after menopause." My eyes narrow on the pair, but they don't cough up the truth.

"Don't you be worrying about us. We are just two old women who sometimes need a good cry."

"Yeah, hmm mmm, okay." Aside from torturing it out of them, something I won't do in front of Layla, I don't know how to get the truth out of them, so I might as well change the subject. "How was Layla today?"

Tina finally calms herself enough to tell me about the tea party they hosted for some of Layla's friends from the library, and then they had a fun afternoon of grocery shopping. I'm sure I'll have a bag or two of new things to take home. They wrap up with Layla lying down for her nap.

The sniffles continue throughout their recollection, and when I begin to pack up Layla to head home.

Aside from the crying and sniffles, they don't act any different from their normal selves. Once I have Layla in her car seat, and we are headed home, I ask her knowing I won't get an answer.

"Do you know what is wrong with those two, baby?"

"Gramma! Mimi!" She claps happily.

I wouldn't have any luck asking Dad or Cord either. Neither of them knows what is going on with their wives half of the time anyway.

So, I give up.

"Are you ready for our slumber party and our fun day tomorrow?"

"Fu!" That little cheer is enough to put a smile on my face and melt the ice from my heart.

Daxon,

Here I am again. Sitting in front of my computer and writing to you. I'm honestly surprised they haven't shut down your email yet. Maybe they see my weekly messages and are leaving it up to help me heal.

I'll never heal from the news that shocked my world. But I've done an okay-ish job living my life in the best way you would want for me.

The funniest, or oddest thing, happened to me today when I picked up Layla from my mom's. For a split second, I thought I smelled you on our little girl, but when I tried to catch it again, it was gone, so I'm sure I was wrong about even picking up on it to begin with.

And then again, our moms were acting strange, stranger than normal, but they wouldn't tell me why. I don't know what's going on.

Layla and I made a blanket fort in the living room tonight and watched some of her favorite movies until she finally crashed on me. I couldn't go to bed until I wrote to you. Tomorrow, we are going up to our spot one last time before the snow starts to stick.

Brooke May

As always, I hope you find your way home.

Love, Mercy

Chapter Fifteen

PACKING A WIGGLING BABY uphill on my back isn't for the faint of heart. Luckily, I increased my workouts after having her. This would be easier, though, if she would quit moving so much.

"We are almost there, Layla." Even though this hike is more like a walk in the park for me now, I'm still dragging in a breath. "Mommy would greatly appreciate it if you would quit moving around so much."

I get it, I really do. Sitting up behind me while I do all the work can't be much fun. She has trees and the random squirrels and chipmunks to look at but nothing else. The ride up here was far more enjoyable for her because we saw a few deer and two moose. I love seeing nature through her eyes. No matter how many times Layla's seen an animal, the excitement coursing through her tiny body makes it seem like the first time.

"Momma!" She bounces. From my periphery, I see her little finger pointing at a squirrel running around a tree.

"Yes, baby." Looking up ahead, I see the sky. That means we are feet away from our destination.

Sweat trickles down my back as we reach the end of our little journey. It wasn't a long hike, but it was enough to cause a sweat to break out on my back under the straps of the carrier. Not only do I have Layla's added weight on my back, but our food and drinks in the compartment under her.

Getting to the spot that is a safe distance from the ledge, I finally stop to put her down and then whistle for Trigger. I have never put him on a leash up here. He knows to come back to us when we call.

Sure enough, I hear the clinging of his tags before he comes through the timber at our back. I don't worry about him getting close to the edge since he has a better case of self-preservation than my child does.

Thankfully, I don't get lost in thoughts when I have her with me. My eyes never wander off her for long, and I tend to keep her behind me or in my arms.

It's surprisingly warm for this time of year. Usually, there is already being a good amount of snow on the ground, but fate has decided to keep it at bay for a little while longer. I'll take it. That means we get this final time up here.

"What are you thinking, Layla?" She bats my hands away when I muss her hair as she continues to play in the dirt between my legs. Smiling, I look out at the scenery before us. Sometimes, I imagine what it would be like if Daxon were here with us. He would have insisted on hauling Layla himself while I brought up the rear with the food and drinks. Who knows, maybe I could have been pregnant again by now. I always wanted my children close in age. Being an only child left me longing for someone to spend time with when I couldn't go outside to play or be near my friends. I never wanted my child to go through the same.

Other times, I think of what this landscape looked like to the first person who set their gaze upon it. How magnificently terrifying it must have been. Going from the flatlands of the prairies to climb something this massive only to look out and see that there is still a ways to go.

An uneasy prickling sensation grips the back of my neck, and awareness grabs me. I'm not foolish enough to think we are up here all by ourselves. There are always people on the mountains and an animal or two somewhere around here.

Holding Layla, I look around. Finding nothing, I'm relieved it's only the three of us. Trigger, who is usually a great watch dog, is quietly chewing on a thick stick he found. If he isn't alerted to anything, then I shouldn't be either.

Rearranging us, I settle back against the base of the tree that holds Daxon's and my initials and just relax. I have my daughter between my legs playing and my dog a few feet away. What more could I ask for?

In the blue sky sprinkled with random white clouds, a face appears. A strong jaw coated in a light dusting of stubble, a firm line for lips, and then the penetrating stare that can read me better than anyone I have ever known.

"Oh, Daxon."

I do my best to keep his memory alive for not only myself but for Layla as well. There is a but lingering in the back of my mind. What if it's time for me to move on?

That question causes untold pain to course through me. I don't like the idea, but maybe it's time. Daxon has been gone for too long. If he hasn't made it home by now, he might not ever. I

Love, Mercy

need to come to terms with the possibility that he will never make it back.

Rubbing my chest, I can't handle this pain, but I must. For my future and the future of my daughter, I need to come to terms with the fact that my husband is gone and I might never get an answer to what happened to him.

Chapter Sixteen

THIS IS WHY I THOUGHT coming down on Sunday would help avoid this from happening.

I'm about ready to pull my hair out. The parade is set to start in thirty minutes, and everything is set to go except the cheerleaders have misplaced the pompoms they made especially for today.

To make matters worse, the graying sky is warning me that doom will be upon us any moment now. I even checked the weather before we left the house, and there was no mention of rain, sleet, or even snow.

"Please just be overcast." Muttering to myself, I look over my clipboard. Everyone is nearly lined up.

Our legion auxiliary is leading the parade with the flags, followed by our small high school marching band, and then each year of military service. The two World War II veterans are both in wheelchairs and will be pushed by a couple of football players who were able and willing to wear the uniforms of those gentlemen.

Love, Mercy

Cheerleaders will be flanking each group, and it won't be complete without their pom-poms.

"Mercy." A panting breath coming from my back has me turning around to find one of my volunteers running to me. I hold my breath, hoping that I don't hear any more bad news.

"Yes?"

"Everyone is ready, but Chase doesn't have his picture."

"Wh-what?" Oh, God. I can't freak out now. I don't have the time for this. Chase has agreed to carry Daxon's picture every year we do this. Him not having it today doesn't feel right.

"He said he couldn't find it. He's sure it's in a box somewhere, but his new house is packed with them ..." Her explanation trails off as I look out at the crowd gathering down the street. So many people have come to celebrate and honor our veterans. My husband's image missing from it isn't going to matter to them.

Taking a shaky step away, I can only nod. I hope she doesn't try to say anything else because I am deaf to it all. Thank God I dropped Layla off with her grandparents once they got here. They have her bundled up from the sudden chill and are likely feeding her hot chocolate and cinnamon rolls right now.

"I need to ..." Trailing off, I start to push my way through the groups lining up for the parade. Once I'm on the other side, I look up to find a cheerleader with her nose in her phone. Pom-poms ... I need to be looking for those.

Straightening myself out, I walk up to her. "Have you seen the pom-poms?"

Her gum pops before she looks up to answer me. "Oh, hi, Mrs. Logan." Her eyes are widened like she didn't catch what I asked her. I'm sure she didn't.

"Have you seen the pompoms?" Repeating myself doesn't ease the restlessness I have swarming inside me.

"Umm ... no?" She cringes. "We had breakfast at the brewery, so maybe they are there?"

"Thanks." She doesn't offer to come with me, and I don't wait for her. Taking off to the next block down, I enter the bustling brewery and search the room. Nothing. It would be easy to spot a mountain of red, white, and blue pompoms anywhere in this building, but they aren't here.

Going to the bar, I impatiently wait for the bartender who is serving coffee rather than beer to get to me.

Love, Mercy

"Need a top off, Mercy?"

"Please." Unscrewing my cap, I slide my mug over to him. "You haven't happened to see the pom-poms, have you?"

He isn't the one to answer me, but the woman sitting next to me. "I was just down at the VFW and there was a pile of them on a table near the back."

I push away from the bar top before my mug is filled again. "Really?" She nods, a small smile brightening her face. "Oh, thank you." After hugging her, I take back my mug and head out the door without paying. I should feel bad about that, but I need to get those pom-poms first.

Rushing back down the street, I end up sprinting past my family in my rush. Somehow, I manage to keep all my coffee in the mug.

I don't pay heed to the fact that someone may be pulling the door open to leave as I burst in. A few people are still here, mainly eating before the parade, as I look around. Scoping out the place, I find them exactly where the kind woman told me they were.

Smiling and waving at the people still here, I march over to them and somehow scoop all of them into my arms. My clipboard is tucked under my arm, and I've had to give up my mug so I can still open the door to head back to the cheerleaders.

I'm half relieved now that I have located these. Now, if only I could quickly locate a picture of Daxon for Chase, then everything would be perfect.

Shoulders relaxing, I close my eyes as I turn and breathe a less edgy lungful of air. I have enough time to locate all the cheerleaders and get to my position. Turning back to the door, I shout over to the one staff member I see.

"Tara Beth, I'll be back for my mug."

"No problem, hun."

Without a moment to spare, I push out the door and quickly locate every cheerleader. It's like one of those picture searches as I find all twelve of them in a matter of minutes.

Thankfully, each of them has forgone their phones and is looking for me. Once my load is delivered, I return to the VFW for my mug and then take my post next to the podium where our announcer is all ready to go.

Love, Mercy

"Morning, Archie." Setting my mug down, I rub my hands together. "Ready to get this show on the road?"

"Absolutely."

Chapter Seventeen

"GOOD MORNING, LADIES AND GENTLEMEN." Archie is the perfect man for this job. His voice booms even without a microphone. "Thank you for braving this sudden chill for our veterans this morning. We promise not to keep you too long."

Cheers sound around us.

"Without further ado, I'll hand you over to our wonderful organizer, Mercy Logan, in prayer."

I didn't want to do this. I'm not one for the spotlight, but everyone on the committee agreed it should be me.

"Good morning, everyone. Thank you for your continued support of our local veterans. Seeing how this has grown so much from last year is awe-inspiring." Once the crowd calms, I say a short prayer for our town, our veterans and their families, and for our active-duty members. The pendant against my chest feels as though it is burning and glowing as I think of Daxon. I thought of him last year when I did this very thing.

Love, Mercy

Handing the microphone back over to Archie, I take a step back, collect my mug, and get ready to see our hard work laid out before us. We are toward the end of the parade route, so it will be a while before everyone reaches us.

The cannon—the very one my dad and father-in-law made—sounds, sending a thrill through each person standing and waiting as the marching band begins to play the national anthem.

Archie speaks of the pride we have for our veterans—past, present, and future—as the line drags down. I'm certain only the people standing next to us can hear him, but it doesn't deter him.

"This year, we wanted to showcase each generation of the military from our sleepy town. All of them are leading up to some of our stateside active duty members. But this year, we have a very special surprise."

What is he talking about?

Frowning, I look up from my mug to see his cheeks are reddened from the chill, but his smile is enough to warm him.

"As you all know, our fearless leader, Mercy, lost her husband last year."

Tears, unbidden, begin to pool in my eyes. I have no clue what is happening. This wasn't organized to focus on me. I don't want the recognition or attention. That belongs to our veterans.

"She's one of the strongest women I have ever had the honor of calling a friend." He turns to me, and so do a few others. "So this year, we went behind her back to put something together for her."

The band grows louder, and I look up to see the legion auxiliary matching our way with the band at their back, but it is Decker, one of Daxon's friends, positioned between our two World War II vets who has my attention.

He's holding a large poster size piece of paper.

Dear Mercy,

Frowning, I'm at a loss.

We all stand and pay our respects to the flags as well as the veterans as they get closer.

Next comes our Korean vets and stationed dead center in front of them is Holt, another close friend. He, too, is holding a sign up.

Love, Mercy

Your words, sometimes lost and other times just as simple as any other conversation, have meant the world to me.

Standing, I abandon my mug and wish I had a pair of binoculars.

When the Vietnam vets come into view, it is yet another friend, Ryder, who leads the charge.

I have been through the pits of hell, but my northern star was always my focus to return.

Tears are flowing now. I don't know where they got these words, but something is yanking on my soul to continue to look beyond.

Duke leads the veterans of Desert Storm.

I couldn't come back until I knew I was as whole of a man as I could be.

"Wh-what's going on, Archie?" My legs begin to grow weak, and I reach for the older man for support.

"The only thing we could think of to thank you for your own dedication." He kisses the top of my head. "Now, watch."

And I do.

I watch as Chase arrives with everyone who has served around and since 9/11 and nearly fall apart.

I'm home, babe. I'm not the man who left you, but I'm still the man who loves you with all his heart and soul.

"Oh, my God." Tears cascade, adding a bite to my chilled cheeks. "Oh, my God."

Like a slow approaching storm, I watch from the distance as people who were seated stand once more, and like far-off thunder, applause follows as three lone people bring up the end of the parade.

A voice breaks through the speakers, and it is then that I notice no one else is talking. Even the band has grown quiet as I see my dad and Cord flanking an extremely familiar person.

"Mercy." My knees tremble at that deep timbre. It's like sex, rippling through every nerve ending my body possesses. "Surprise."

Most of our small town knows what I have been through and worried for me after news of Daxon's fate spread.

Love, Mercy

"You always said you wanted a surprise like you watch and cry over on YouTube." I can feel his grin. "And here it is, babe."

He reaches me, and I don't think I ever thought I could vault over a railing like this before. I sprint into his arms, my tears blocking most of my vision, but I could find him in a pitch-black cave. Our bodies slam together as I fall apart and cling to him because I'm never letting go again.

Chapter Eighteen

"YOU'RE REALLY HERE?"

"I told you," he murmurs to me as a thunderous applause storms around us. "I will always find my way back to you."

"Where have you been?"

"Through hell, babe, and I needed to get my mind back before I could return to you and be the husband and father you and Layla need."

Pulling back, I take him in. He is thinner. There is a gaunt horror to his appearance that tells me all I need to know. He has lived through something horrific.

He is still as handsome as the day it dawned on me that I was meant to be with him. I'm floored by all questions speaking at once in my head that a headache is starting to slam into the front of my head. It isn't welcomed. Not when my heart is pounding as if I just ran a marathon nonstop. Ice and heat fight to take hold of my body as I stand there and stare at him.

"Thank God. You're not going anywhere from now on."

Love, Mercy

He chuckles, and it is like the sound of angels singing because that's just what he is.

"I'm not going anywhere."

While I'm lost in the moment with him, I forget about everyone else until I feel someone pull on my leg.

"Momma?"

Pushing away from my tight hold of Daxon, I give Layla a watery smile.

"You cry?"

"Happy tears, baby." Picking her up, I place a hand on Daxon's chest. The beat of his heart underneath is reassuring to feel the steady rhythm. Looking at her and then to her daddy, I find him wide-eyed, and if I'm not mistaken, nervous. "Layla, this is your daddy."

"Dada?"

"Yep. He went away to be a superhero." It's the easiest way to explain this to her at this age. She will grow up with a better understanding, but for now, all she needs to know is he is a superhero. "And now he is home to help me protect you."

It might be due to his pictures being a constant in her life, but she doesn't hesitate to jump from my arms to his.

"Dada!"

"Hey, little one. It's nice to meet you finally." He squeezes her as tears fall from his own eyes. "Mommy has sent me pictures of you and I feel like I know you already, but I'm looking forward to knowing you better."

He kisses the crown of her head before looking back at me.

"But first, Mommy and I have some things to talk about."

Now I'm nervous. I know he can see all the questions I have swarming in my mind, and like always, he wants to give me all the answers he is allowed to give.

"I'm ready if you are."

"That's why I'm home. As healed as I could get, I won't be complete until I fill in the blanks you deserve."

Reluctantly, Daxon hands our daughter over to his dad before grabbing my hand and leading me away.

"I've already talked to your boss and cleared your schedule for the day."

Love, Mercy

"Oh?" He doesn't say another word until we are in my car and heading to our house. He is driving, but there is an edge to him that wasn't there before. Whatever he has been through has changed him. I know he would never do anything to break us or hurt our daughter he has yet to truly know. It pains me to leav her behind, but he didn't give me much of a choice.

"Quit gnawing on that lip of yours. I don't want to see you wince when I kiss you." Butterflies return to my stomach and chest after a long hibernation.

"Now that sounds like my Daxon." I do my best to lighten the air, but I don't think that is going to happen until we talk.

"I'm still me, Mercy, just slightly bent now." Reaching over, he captures my hand once more and places a gentle kiss on it.

We don't speak again until we are in our home. He walks in like he never left. The house hasn't changed too much. The furniture is still the same, but the desktop computer has been replaced with a laptop, and there are toys everywhere.

Falling onto the couch, he moves only to pull a dinosaur from under him.

"Sorry, Layla has kind of taken over the house. She has so many toys and I don't know what to do with most of them."

"Don't ever apologize for living your life, Mercy," he growls, and I take a step back. He has never taken that tone with me before. And then he sighs. "Come here, babe. I didn't mean to snap."

I need to remind myself that he was on a mission when he went missing. Obviously, he went through hell wherever he was and is still trying to recover. There is a high likelihood that he may have PTSD now, and I need to be there to support him, not cower away and ignore it.

"Right." Going over to him, I fall onto the cushion next to him. "I'm okay." Placing a hand on his arm, I watch him flinch, causing my heart to ache.

It takes him a minute; he plays around with the dinosaur before he places it on the coffee table and turns to me. He dives into the depths of a mission gone bad. He and two others were captured while everyone else was left to die alone in the desert. They were tortured and left on the edge of death time after time only to be brought back enough to be tormented once more.

He lost track of time and his mind for long periods of time until his captors made a mistake. They let one of them loose, thinking he was on the verge of death, and it would have been easier to haul him out once he was dead. His companion had just enough strength left in his weak body to set the other two free and was the distraction while Daxon and the other man escaped.

They didn't know where they were or who to trust, so they took off after securing some food and water. They got lost and wandered. His partner didn't make it even after they found sanctuary. It was still some time before the military was able to recover him and the body of his fallen companion. And still some time after that to verify his identity. He had no identification, no way to prove who he was until he was detained and put through the wringer.

His story is almost impossible to believe, but the serious note to his voice and the hard glare he has pinned to the wall behind me conveys the truth. My hand has found its way to my necklace, and I tighten my grip around it.

"By the time I got back to the US, they kept me isolated for medical clearance. I wasn't allowed to contact anyone because of the severity of what I went through and the mission I was supposed to succeed with. Guilt consumed me, Mercy. It still does. I'm the only survivor. I should have done everything in my power to get those men out and home safely, but I failed them. I failed you by not coming home—"

"You failed no one, Daxon." I stop him from further damning himself. "You did what you could with the situation you found yourself in. Those men did the same." I didn't need to be there to know that.

He falls silent, and I don't know what else to say to make this better. I'm sure they didn't let him leave until a therapist saw him, and as much as I want to ask, I won't.

"Your emails ..." He begins, licking his lips before looking at me once more. "I read every single one of them you sent."

"You read them?" The question stumbles out.

"My therapist thought it would help me heal. At first, more guilt weighed on me because I missed all of it, but then I saw what I was being told. I had a life waiting for me at the only home I have ever had." He grabs me, pulling me onto his lap, and the warmth I have longed for is welcomed back around my body. "I'm far from being healed, Mercy, but I'm here, and I know I will get better with your help and that of our family and friends as well as getting to know our little girl more than just what I've read."

A sob erupts out of me as I latch onto his front and bury my face into his chest.

Love, Mercy

All of it; his captivity, his survival, his struggle to return home to me doesn't have me breaking down, but builds me up instead. I have to be strong for both of us and be there for him when he needs me most. We still have a long road ahead of us to get back to us—to get him back—but I'm ready for that. I will help this man through anything.

Daxon has returned home to me.

Chapter Nineteen

OUR LIPS FUSE AS recognition of one another, and the memories of all the times we have locked in our lover's embrace flood back to us.

My hunger for him, the insatiable need to unite with him once more has reason falling by the wayside as I quickly disrobe.

I don't know how much time we will have together before our family shows up to celebrate his miracle return to us.

His hunger and need match my own. Fumbling, we remove all articles of clothing. My heated eyes look at every part of him, and I do my best not to react to the scars marring his body.

My God, what did they do to you?

I won't voice that unless he wants to talk about it, but to me, it feels like it would reopen wounds that he has claimed to heal from.

I'm separated from him for a few seconds as we remove our pants. His erection, hard and throbbing, presses against my slickness as I sit back down on his lap. Lust, love, hunger, long-awaited reunion throws any form of foreplay away as I lift and guide him into me.

It feels foreign while at the same time reminds me of home as I fully seat myself on his lap and pause to revel at this moment.

As I begin to move, his hands run up and down my body from my waist to cup my breasts, and it doesn't feel like any time has passed since the last time we were together.

Our gaze breaks only to blink. Otherwise, we stay fixated on one another as we relearn the other all over again.

There is nothing rushed about this.

His erection pulsates within me as I tighten around him. A benefit of having a child and learning workouts to help return my body to the way it used to be. My inner muscles are stronger than ever.

"Sweet, Jesus, Mercy." His head may be thrown back, but his eyes never break from mine. His Adam's apple bobs as he keeps a loose hold on his control.

This first time is for me to control. The gentle pace of lovemaking is bringing us back together in a carnal way before he takes hold of me. He will leave my voice hoarse from screaming the house down, and my legs like Jell-O as my body becomes spent.

"Oh, Daxon." I moan, gyrating and rolling my body so he will hit every spot that has my mind reeling.

As gentle as this is, I'm still falling apart as if he has me bent over the back of the couch, my hair fisted in his hand, and is slamming into me from behind.

My body straightens as if I'm a rocket about ready to take off as my orgasm takes full control of my body and mind. Daxon's hands roughly grab my hips as he too shoots up and into me. His roar is so loud that I'm sure the neighbors can hear him if they are home.

I'm sucking in as much air as I can as I come back to my right mind. Opening my eyes, I feel a small smile spread across my face. He mimics me perfectly.

Leaning closer to him, I cup his strong face, and though I miss the muscle he once had, I'm just glad to have him whole and home.

"Welcome home, soldier. I love you more than anything aside from Layla."

                                    Love, Mercy

"I love you, too, Mercy."

Chapter Twenty

Daxon

I NEVER THOUGHT I would be able to find comfort again.

Resting in the middle of the bed Mercy and I share, I have my wife on one side and my daughter on the other. Both are cuddled close to me as the winter winds pick up outside. Over each pec, I have a slumbering head breathing in even breaths.

My world fell apart the day it all went bad, and it wasn't easy to get to here. Some days, even when I was freed and somewhere safe to recover, I didn't think I would make it. Suicidal thoughts took hold of me far more than I will ever tell Mercy.

Not that I have any plans of ever letting her know how dark I went before I could find the light of her star again.

It was six months into my delicate recovery when my therapist told me about the emails, and as I logged in with a password I'd never forget, I cried when I saw the number waiting there for me.

Love, Mercy

I fell apart at first, seeing how destroyed Mercy was of my news and her worry not knowing what happened or even if I were alive. I read them all in one sitting and reread them over and over again whenever she sent a new one.

As I grew stronger, not only physically but mentally, it felt like I hadn't missed as much as I really did.

Mercy did a great job making sure I knew everything going on in her and Layla's life, including so many pictures that if I had a phone, I would have used up all the memory to save each one.

I still live with the guilt. That won't go away anytime soon, but I can live with it for the most part.

Layla stirs, her tiny hand fisting into my drool-soaked shirt as she murmurs something and settles once more.

God, I've missed so much yet don't really feel like I have.

As I turn to face Mercy, her peaceful face helps me find some as well. Yet not enough to fall back asleep just yet.

She shifts and exposes her necklace, the very one she promised never to take off, and it seems she's kept her promise. One of the pictures she sent me of Layla's birth show she even wore it while having our child.

That's one of the reasons I have one in my bag for Layla. It isn't a big as Mercy's, but she is now one of my guiding stars as well. I will give one to any other daughter we have. I'll have to figure something out for sons if they are to come in the hopefully near future.

Taking in a deep breath, I look at the ceiling.

"I'm home, and it was all because of Mercy's love." She is the true embodiment of her name and I love her more each day for her kind heart.

Epilogue

Daxon

One Year Later

MERCY'S GLORIOUS BODY WRITHES under me. Her lips are parted as she takes in a staggering breath as I slam into her over and over again.

Complete, I am complete in this connection with my woman, my savior, one half of my entire world.

It's been one hell of a year, but this right here has made the mental battle I've been through so much more victorious.

"Daddy! Daddy! Daddy!" Layla's little voice has no place in the memory of what I did to her mother last night.

Looking up from my workbench, I can't fight back the instant smile that slams onto my face as my little girl bounds over to me.

It's taken me time to accept the unconditional love this little girl has for me. Just like her mom, she has embraced every broken part of me and mended them back together. Her love and that from Mercy has been just what I needed.

Once winter was gone and spring was in full bloom, I built my workshop in our backyard where I make custom log furniture. I found that messing around with wood has helped give me a concentration I lacked after getting home. It has allowed me to be available for my girls, family, and friends.

"What's goin' on, princess?" Putting down my pencil and triangle, I don't have a moment to dust myself off before she is launching herself at me.

"Here, Daddy." She giggles as I rub my face against hers. She produces a piece of paper.

"What's this?" I say with a surprised voice that doesn't sound anything like me, but she loves it. "Is this another beautiful picture for me to put up?"

"No." She giggles. "Mommy."

"Oh, Mommy has a note for me?"

She nods, her wild hair flying everywhere.

Love, Mercy

"Well, let's see what Mommy has to say." Putting her down, I make sure the table saw is unplugged before I read the note from my wife. Only need that to happen once to have a rapid series of heartaches to warn me away from ever leaving something plugged in with Layla around

Mercy has never given up on writing letters to me. Sometimes, they still come in from email. Those ones are usually written while she is at work, but mostly, I'm subjected to her horrible handwriting. That doesn't matter to me, though. Knowing she still tells me random things she could easily say in person warms me to the point that might rival the heat of the sun.

It has also helped in my healing process.

Daxon,

You say that my emails led you back to us and that the notes I leave you now have helped to heal you even more. I hope I can continue writing these, and that even in old age and a weak mind, I will remember to write something to you.

A line or two is all we need sometimes, and others, they are much longer.

I love you and the strength you have to allow yourself to get the help you need to heal from what you went through and

your courage to keep your head held high each day. You are more than the man I fell in love with, and more than you were yesterday. You are a great man, a wonderful husband, and an amazing father.

That's why I'm writing to you now. I'm sitting in the kitchen rather than cleaning it and watching you working away outside.

I know you hold onto many regrets, one of them is not being here for my pregnancy and all of Layla's firsts. Well, babe, I'm glad to tell you that you don't have to miss round two. You get to be here for us ... the three of us.

I'm sure you're smiling like a madman now. In fact, I'm watching and waiting for it. Now get your sexy ass inside so we can celebrate all our good fortune.

You've returned to us and get to live out the life we have created in this world.

Love, Mercy

Note from the Author

Dear Reader,

I wanted to write a different kind of romance with Daxon and Mercy. Instead of starting with them falling in love, I wanted to share their story after their Happily Ever After. I hope I brought justice to what military families can go through.

Love,

Brooke

Acknowledgements

Always and forever, first and foremost, I thank God for giving me this gift and the courage to put my stories out there into the world.

To the men and women of our Armed Forces, thank you for being our superheroes, for going above and beyond every day for not only the people of our country, but the world. You make a difference.

The warden and boys; thank you so much for making my life anything but easy. You three keep me on my toes, give me strange inspiration, and I would be lost without you.

My family; thank you for always being around when I need someone to bounce ideas off of. Mom, you were my first cheerleader with my imagination. Thank you for listening to whatever concept I was trying to work for. Dad, thank you for teaching me a lot of what I'm using in this series. Without your mountain man ways, I wouldn't know the details of the animals like I do.

Thank you, Marie, Brittany, Lindsay, Avery, K.R., Sandra, and Jaime for joining me with this series. Y'all are a wonderful bunch of ladies and hope we can work together again down the road.

Jenny, thank you for being the amazing editor you are. I feel I've learned and grown since My Cowboy and I hope to continue to grow but not too much because I will always need you.

Tracie, once more you have made an amazing cover that I knew right away was for my book. I absolutely love this one. I love every one you've made for me, but this one makes me sigh. Dark Water Covers is the best!

To every single blogger and fellow author out there, thank you for doing what you love. Thank you for inspiring me with your written words and for the bloggers who love to read and spread their love to everyone they can.

And, of course, to you the reader, thank you for finding my book and reading it. Thank you for taking a chance. Without you, none of this would be possible. Thank you for your support, your reviews, wonderful words, and your encouragement.

About the Author

Born and raised in Northern Wyoming. Brooke spent a great deal of her childhood and even well into her adulthood in her imagination and creating different stories. With an overactive imagination life has been truly entertaining.

A mother of two wild and reckless boys and a wife; Brooke keeps busy year round doing things with her pups and family. When she isn't writing, can usually be spotted walking somewhere in town, at the library with her youngest, or up in the mountains four-wheeling, hiking, fishing, and some hunting. A notebook and camera are never far from her side when she is out on her adventures with her family.

She loves hearing from readers and anyone who feels like talking. Feel free to pay her a visit whenever.

Sign up for Brooke's mailing list for information on new releases at:

http://brookemayauthor.weebly.com/

Stalk Brooke:

https://www.facebook.com/authorbrookemay

http://www.twitter.com/B_May88

http://instagram.com/brookemay_author

https://www.pinterest.com/authorbrookemay/

Books by Brooke

My Cowboy Series:

    My Cowboy

    Faith in My Cowboy

    Loved by My Cowboy

    My Cowgirl

The Predator Series:

    The Predator Part One

    The Predator Part Two

    The Predator Wildfire Knockout

    Back in the Ring

Moto X Series:

    Roosted

    Cased

    Pinned

Powder River Pack Series:

    A Second Chance

Code of Honor Series:

    Courage of Us

    Love, Mercy

Coming soon:

Call of the Alpha: Powder River Pack Book Two, early 2020

Bottoming Out: Moto X Book Four, summer 2020

Honoring Those Who Serve

For the rest of the books in the series, look up the following authors.

Never Forget by Marie Savage

Public Relations by Brittany Anne

Broken Heartbeats by Lindsay Becs

Plane Love by Avery Kingston

Saving Ryleigh by K.R. Reese

Callahan's Haven by Sandra Daniels

Signed Sealed Delivered by Jaime Russell

Hidden Letters by Audrey Ravine

Made in the USA
Columbia, SC
07 November 2022